At Your Service
Book Three

By C. L. Porter

Subscribe to C. L. Porter's Mailing List

Sign up for my newsletter at http://eepurl.com/_VtsL to receive exclusive updates about incoming titles and to be the first to get your hands on the new releases (including free advance reader copies for readers willing to write a review).

CONTENTS

Subscribe to C. L. Porter's Mailing List 2

Chapter 1 4

Chapter 2 18

Chapter 3 33

Chapter 4 54

Chapter 5 69

Chapter 6 79

Chapter 7 91

Chapter 8 115

Chapter 9 128

Epilogue 139

Subscribe to C. L. Porter's Mailing List 143

Books by C. L. Porter 144

Chapter 1

OLIVIA

"Why did you do it?" I asked Max.

We sat in a small, quiet café in the center of the town. I insisted on the meeting in a public place. I no longer trusted him after what I saw in the office. Max had been a dangerous man. I should have known better.

"Do what? Are you talking about Tim? I only advised him to tell Courtney the truth."

"I'm talking about what you did at the office. Are you out of your mind?"

"I have no idea what you're talking about, Olivia. I swear."

"You swear? And what about Tim? Is he really a golf coach, or perhaps your colleague?"

"Courtney told you."

"She did. And you hadn't said a word earlier. Why?"

"What was I supposed to do? Tim wanted to tell Courtney himself. If I told you, you would have told her. And you didn't tell me about Courtney's job, either."

He shouldn't have lied to me about Tim's job, and it wasn't right to lie to him about Courtney. But it didn't matter now. If he lied about his friend, he probably lied about his involvement with what happened at the agency's office, too.

"That's beside the point now. Why did you break into the office and point everything at me?"

"Olivia, I really don't know what you're talking about. I wanted to speak with Victoria before your meeting, but Tim told me something that changed my mind."

"Like hell he did. Max, do you realize you ruined my life?"

"I didn't do anything, Olivia. You have to believe me." He placed his hand on mine. I still craved this man, but I couldn't stand his touch at this moment.

"Please take your hand off mine, Max."

"Olivia…"

"Please."

He took his hand away and raked it in his hair. He had bloodshot eyes, as if he had skipped a night of sleep. All the proof pointed at him.

"I didn't do it, Olivia."

"It's hard to believe you after our conversation yesterday. Let me quote you: 'I'll find a way to get you out of this business.' That's what you told me yesterday. I go to the office today and Victoria tells me I'll never work as an escort anymore. Convenient, isn't it?"

"Tell me exactly what happened."

"For what? So that you can come up with new lies? I spoke with a neighbor. She described someone eerily similar to you wandering around the office in the morning. Were you checking out if Victoria found the mess you left there?"

"I was in the neighborhood, but I didn't do anything. I swear."

"I'm sorry, but I can't believe you. Nobody else had any reason to pull this shit on me."

"Please tell me what happened, Olivia."

"I don't want to talk with you, Max. You don't even know how you fucked up my life."

"Please. If you don't want to see me for a couple weeks, fine. But let me find out the truth. I'll bring you the proof and show you it wasn't me."

I sighed. Why did Max have to have this effect on me? Even when I was mad at him, I couldn't say no. "Fine."

He leaned his face forward.

"I went to the office to talk with Victoria about my return. The whole place was messed up. Overturned furniture, stuff flying in the air. And there was a piece of paper that said if I ever worked as an escort again, you would burn the office and hunt down Victoria's family."

"It wasn't me. Do you honestly believe I would be so fucked up to do this shit? I'm an escort, not a fucking criminal."

"If you find the proof it wasn't you, bring it to me. Otherwise, leave me alone for a couple weeks. What you said yesterday... I don't want this kind of control in my life. And I have other stuff on my plate. I need to find another job if I don't want to starve."

"I can give you some m—"

"No. I'm not going to accept any money from you."

"Fine. I'll show you it wasn't me. I promise." He rose up, kissed me on the forehead and left.

I desperately wanted to believe it wasn't him, but there was no reason to think otherwise. I shoved the thought aside. I had a more pressing issue now. I was almost broke and I could no longer work as an escort.

One hour later, I was back at home staring at the wall. I sat on the bed with Luna purring in my lap. She had always calmed me down, but the shit that happened today was beyond anything I had experienced so far.

I didn't want to ask the clinic for a refund. There was nobody in the world who deserved the surgery more than my mom. I wouldn't disappoint her, even if she still hadn't known I paid for her treatment without asking her first.

I dialed Mom's number.

"Hello, darling," she said in a happy, warm voice. "How are you?"

Oh, God, how much I loved her. I regretted that she lived so far away, but there were no opportunities for me back in Montpelier, Vermont. The cold weather didn't help much, either.

"I'm fine, Mom. I need to speak with you about something."

"Tell me. Is everything all right?"

"It's about your arthritis."

"What about it? If you can't afford the meds any longer, it's fine. I'll manage, honey."

"It's about the new treatment. Auntie told me about it."

There was silence in the phone. "I didn't want you to know about it."

"Why, Mom? You know I would do anything for you."

"That's precisely the reason why. I don't want to ruin your life because you decided to cover my expensive surgery. I'm an old woman. It makes no sense to treat me."

"Mom, you're sixty-two. I… I want you to hold my kids, be a grandmother. If you don't have the surgery, you won't be able to tie your shoes in a year or two."

Mom sobbed into the phone. My throat tightened. I couldn't afford to break down.

"If I decide to have the surgery, will you come home?"

"I will, Mom."

"With your lovely boyfriend?"

The thought of losing Max pierced my heart, but I couldn't forgive him if it was he who ruined my career as an escort.

"I… If his schedule allows, we'll come together."

"I will repay you every single cent, sweetheart."

"Mom, please, stop. Paying for this surgery won't even repay you for all the things you did for me. When Dad died…" I couldn't hold it any longer. Tears trickled down my cheeks and my hands shook.

"I love you, Olivia. I will do it for you, honey."

"Please speak with Auntie. Let her handle the surgery. And don't be mad at her. She made the right choice telling me about it."

"I'm sorry, Olivia. I feel so bad hiding it from you."

"It's fine, Mom. Everything will be all right. I love you."

"I love you, too."

I put the phone away and gazed at Luna playing with a piece of twine on the floor. Sometimes I wished I was a cat. Life would be so much simpler.

I reached for the phone again and dialed Courtney's number. After several rings, I hung up. She had probably already started her shift at the night club.

There was one more person I could ask for help, but I wasn't ready for this step yet. I would wait for Courtney and find out if she could help me get a job as a stripper. If not, I would make the call that would fuck up my life forever.

If I had enough guts to take the job, of course.

MAX

I knew it was a mistake to speak with Olivia about changing her job. If I hadn't asked her about it the day before the appointment, I wouldn't be the first person on her list of suspects.

Now I had a huge problem on my plate. I was as close to being a private investigator as Tim was to being a golf coach, but there was no other way to make Olivia trust me again. I had to find the person who blackmailed Victoria.

I left the café and drove straight to the agency's office. I parked my car in the driveway of the small one-bedroom beige-painted house I saw that morning. A teenager on a skateboard passed me on the sidewalk. He gazed at me with a suspicious expression on his face. It was peppered with acne.

I walked the steps of the porch and knocked on the door. A thirty-something brunette with curly hair and black glasses opened the door.

"How can I help you?" she said.

"I'm looking for Victoria, the manager of your… agency."

She examined my face and glanced at my Mercedes parked in the driveway. "Who are you?"

"I'm Layla's boyfriend. I believe we have the same goal."

"Let him in," an unpleasant, raspy voice said.

The brunette sighed and opened the door ajar. "Come in."

I walked into a huge living room that had been transformed into an office. There were stacks of paper in one corner of the room. A large black desk, a bookshelf and a black leather sofa were overturned. Parts of a smashed printer littered the floor around the desk.

A tall, slim woman with short red hair and pursed lips crouched beside the bookshelf and collected the papers that lay under it.

"Holy shit," I said. "What happened here?"

"What do you think?" the woman said. "We had a nice party and some of us got carried away, Mr. Stranger."

"I'm sorry for my manners. I should have introduced myself. I'm Max Moreira. Layla is my girlfriend."

She rose up and extended her hand.

"Victoria Nelson."

Her hand was as cold as her dark green eyes, but when I smiled at her, her face relaxed. Being a handsome man certainly had its perks at times.

"Layla thinks it was me who made this mess. But I swear it wasn't me, even though I really want her out of this business."

"You're a smart guy, Max. She doesn't belong here. I need tougher girls than her."

"I didn't do it."

"Then who did?" she asked, distrust on her face.

"Who do you think did it?" I asked.

"Someone who didn't want her working as an escort. If it really wasn't you, perhaps a close friend or a family member?"

"Her family doesn't know and her close friend... she's a stripper."

"Anyone else who knows she's an escort?"

"I have no idea. What about her colleagues? You're her new boss, right? Was she close with her ex-boss?"

"Not so close that Alexis would pull off this shit. Besides, Layla's ex-boss is a close friend of the owner of this place. She wouldn't do it."

"Who else, then?"

"I have no idea. Layla hasn't really socialized with the rest of the workers in the agency. She hasn't spoken with anyone from here in the last four weeks, except for me."

I nodded. I gave her plenty of entertainment to make her forget about work.

"Thanks for your help, Victoria. If you remember anything, let me know. I really want to find out who did this."

"I'm on it, but I don't care about Layla either way. I'm not going to let her work here and will discourage other agencies from taking her on. She's arrogant and irresponsible."

"Fine. Just help me find who did it. The rest is between you and Layla."

I shook her hand and left the office. I walked to my Mercedes. The teenager on a skateboard stood by the hood. He took a selfie.

"You like it?" I asked.

He jumped and turned around. "I'm sorry. I didn't meant to touch your car."

"It's fine. I'm Max." I extended my hand.

"Jacob."

"Nice to meet you, Jacob. You're a Mercedes fan?"

"I love German cars, dude. This one is a true beauty. Almost like the one I saw parked here last night."

"Last night? When?"

"I couldn't sleep so I took my board for a ride around two in the morning. Damn, what a sweet ass black W212 it was."

"Who was driving it?"

"The black guy who works here, or used to work here. Yesterday was the first time I saw him here in over a month."

"Do you know his name? Have you spoken with him?"

"No fucking way, man. He's a fucking huge dude. He would have killed me if I said a word to him."

"Thanks, man. Wanna take a ride with me?"

"Holy shit, man. Sure I would."

"Hop inside. I'll take you for a ride around the block."

Twenty minutes later, I dropped Jacob by his house. It was a couple homes away from the office. I parked in the driveway of the agency's office again and knocked on the door. Nobody replied. I waited for a minute or so and rang at the door. I pushed on the knob. The door was locked.

Fuck, I should have gone back to the office first and then expressed my gratitude to Jacob. Whoever the black guy was, he was responsible for driving Olivia away from me.

I pulled out my phone and dialed Olivia's number. If I couldn't meet with her, at least I could fix something else.

Chapter 2

OLIVIA

I woke up at eleven in the morning with a headache that felt like a knife stabbing me in the head. Luna lay by my side on her back, oblivious to the fact that if I didn't find a job soon, I couldn't afford to buy her food.

I got out of bed and took a shower. I tied my hair in a ponytail and sat on the porch with a cup of tea in my hand and my cell phone on the table. Courtney usually ended her shift at four or five in the morning and woke up around noon.

She had to help me get a job. I couldn't work in a cubicle and live hand to mouth. My body was my greatest asset and my only shot to make more than starvation money. I still wanted to buy my mom a home in Phoenix. She deserved to spend her retirement in a nice, warm place, not a hellhole in Vermont. An office job would never let me achieve that goal.

My phone buzzed a couple minutes past noon.

"You called me," Courtney said in a dry voice.

"How are you, Courtney?"

"Fine, I guess. Enjoying my freshly attained single status."

"You really should talk with Tim."

"And hear more bullshit about selling my body? Nope. I'll limit myself to random fucks here and there. How's your job?"

"Not good. I... got fired and my career as an escort is pretty much finished."

"What? Why?"

"Long story. I don't really want to bother you with my problems now, but I need to ask you a favor, Courtney."

"You need to tell me what happened."

"Not now, please. But I have a favor to ask."

"Anything. Tell me what you need." Her voice changed from dry to energetic, eager to help.

"I need to find a new job. Can you ask around, see if I can work as a stripper in your club or somewhere else?"

"Olivia, with all due respect, I don't think that's a good idea for you."

"Why's that?"

"It's a tough job. I know you can handle yourself, but the shit that's been going down there recently is really not for your level."

"Why do all people have to treat me like a kid?"

"What are you talking about?"

"Never mind. Can you help me get a job or not?"

She sighed. "I'll ask around and let you know."

"Thanks. I appreciate it. And… I'm sorry."

"How's Max? Did you speak with him?"

"I did. I don't really want to go into details now, but… we stopped seeing each other."

"Fuck, Olivia. Out of you and me, it's you who deserves a normal relationship with a guy."

"It's a complicated thing. We'll talk later, okay?"

"Fine."

"And you need to fix your problems with Tim."

"I don't want to lie to you, Olivia. I don't see it happening."

"It will. I'm sure of that."

"Yeah. I need to go. I'll let you know when I learn something about the job."

She hung up. I put the phone back on the table and took in a long breath. Courtney's tone made it pretty clear I didn't have a huge chance getting a job as a stripper at her club. I wasn't looking forward to visiting other clubs. This business was dirtier than escort services, and I wasn't in the mood to negotiate with mobsters.

I browsed through my contact list and found the name I was looking for. My finger lingered on the "call" button. I grabbed my cup of cold tea and gulped it down. I was about to click "call" when my phone rang. Max's name was on the screen.

"What part of 'I need distance' don't you understand?" I said.

"I'm sorry I'm calling you, but I didn't want Tim to know. Could you text me Courtney's number?"

"What for?"

"I want to fix what happened between them."

I moved my fingers through my hair. Could I trust him enough not to fuck it up even more?

"I don't think I should give it to you."

"Then give me a better idea of how to fix it. Tim isn't going to call her, and Courtney isn't going to call him. They're both too stubborn for that even though it was a simple misunderstanding."

"A misunderstanding? Him asking her if she had been selling her body?"

"He just wanted to know, Olivia. He doesn't mind her job, whether she's a stripper or a... an escort."

"I won't give you her number, but I want the same thing as you. I'll speak with Courtney, you'll speak with Tim."

"What do you have in mind?"

I told him my plan. Max agreed it was a great idea. I won't lie to you – I actually enjoyed planning it with Max over the phone, even though my trust for him hovered around zero.

When we finished discussing the plan, I hung up. I saw the contact name I was about to call and shuddered. I clicked "cancel." I would give Courtney one full day before making the call.

I strolled around the house thinking about other options for a career switch when my phone rang again. It was Courtney.

"I called DeShawn. He wants to speak with you today at six."

"Oh my God. Thank you so much, Courtney."

"I still think it's a bad idea. I've been doing this for a long time. This is a completely different job than being an escort."

"I guess I'll find it out on my own."

"If you decide to go through with it, I'll help you out. I'll be at your place at five thirty."

Courtney pulled into my driveway at five twenty. I fixed my hair and applied my most expensive perfume to my neck. I had to make a great first impression if I wanted to have a shot at getting this new job.

"Look at you, making yourself so pretty for a job interview," Courtney said in a teasing tone.

"It's all about the first impression, baby."

"Yeah." She turned around and hung her head.

We left my house and got into her car.

"How are you doing, Courtney?"

"I'm doing fine. I miss him, but it will pass soon," she said as she pulled onto the street.

"I have an idea where we can go tomorrow, help you forget about him for a while."

She shot me a quick glance. "What place?"

"It's a surprise. You'll enjoy it, I promise."

"Okay."

"Now, about DeShawn… What should I tell him? What is he going to ask me?"

"Not much. He just wants to see you and make sure you look right for the job. At this point, it's pretty much guaranteed you'll get the job until you piss him off."

"What pisses him off?"

"People who owe him shit and people who boss him around. Be a nice girl, don't argue with him, and you'll be hired. But the shit that will happen at the job… We'll need to talk before you start working."

"Okay. Thank you for doing this, Courtney."

"One more thing."

"What is it?"

"DeShawn is a really crude guy. Don't show him it bothers you or he won't deal with you."

"Okay."

"Now you need to tell me what happened between you and Max."

"It's a long story."

"Long story my ass, Olivia. It's a twenty minute ride to the club. You have plenty of time to tell me everything."

I told her about my conversation with Max the day before my appointment with Victoria and what happened at the office. Then I mentioned his bloodshot eyes, his nervousness around me and his confession that he was there.

"Do you think it was him?" she asked.

"Who else could it be?"

"No idea."

"That's exactly my point."

"It's a bit harsh that you're making him prove his innocence, though."

"I have to get away from him for a while. I'm not sure I want to be with a man who wants to control my life."

"He's worried about you, girl. It's understandable he doesn't want you to work as an escort with all this shit happening lately. Have you heard about the girl attacked a couple days ago?"

"What girl?"

"A john beat a luxurious escort into a coma. She was working on her own. If it wasn't for the guest in the other room, she might have died."

"That's fucked up."

"Max has a good reason to protect you. I wouldn't cut him out even if it was really him. He did it because he cares about you."

***

I can count the times I had been to Black Cat on one hand. I had never enjoyed partying, let alone partying at a seedy night club with strippers, many of whom doubled as hookers.

Working as an escort should have got me used to working with sleazy types. However, there was a world of difference between working as an expensive call girl and working as a stripper in a cheap night club. Aside from a few exceptions, my clientele had been mostly upscale, affluent guys. At the club, the majority of patrons were rednecks and brutes, many of whom had gang affiliations and questionable ethics.

Courtney had a point that I didn't have experience dealing with such types, but I wouldn't let it stand in the way. I needed money too much to care about such things.

Black Cat was your typical seedy strip club. There was a pole in the center of the room, tables and red lounge chairs all over the place, and a long bar with bottles of alcohol lining the shelves. Blue and red lighting finished the design.

I followed Courtney through the back door. In front of us, there was a long, narrow hallway with a couple doors on the left side. A seven-foot tall dark-skinned bodyguard in a tight black t-shirt that emphasized his muscular build stood by the door at the end of the hall.

"Hey, Courtney," he said.

"Hey, Malik. Is DeShawn waiting for us?"

"Yeah. He's a little busy," he said, and smiled, "but he told me to let you in."

Courtney shot me a brief glance. "You ready?"

"Sure."

Malik opened the door. We entered a spacious dark-red-painted room with a large antique mahogany desk at the end of the room. There was a huge black leather sofa at our right and a bookshelf with stacks of paper on the left side. The room smelled of weed and cigarettes.

DeShawn sat in a black leather armchair beside the sofa. He was dressed in a tailored purple suit. A naked blond girl in red high heels kneeled in front of him. Her head moved up and down, followed by her quiet moans.

"Welcome, ladies. Sit down." He motioned to the sofa by his side.

"We can wait outside," I said, confused by the sight.

"No," Courtney said and squeezed my hand. She glared at me and jerked her chin to the sofa. "DeShawn wants to speak with us now."

"Take it balls deep, bitch. Just like that," DeShawn said to the blond girl. He lifted his head and looked at us. "I'll be done in a sec."

We sat on the sofa. I was thankful to Courtney, who gave me the place closest to the door. I was far away from being a prude, but being in the same room with my potential boss and a woman sucking his cock was beyond uncomfortable.

DeShawn pressed the woman's head against his body. She picked up the tempo. Her long blond hair obstructed the view of what she was doing between his legs, but it was awkward, nonetheless.

"Oh, yes. You're so good at this, hoe," he growled. "I'm goin' to come in your mouth now."

He raked his fingers in her hair and arched his back. He groaned and sent me a nasty, wide smile.

Courtney was right. I had no idea what I was getting myself into.

When he was done blowing his load inside the woman's mouth, he pulled her away and zipped his pants. She wiped her mouth and stood up. He smacked her in the ass.

"Time to go, hoe. I'll fuck your pussy later."

The blond turned around. She shot me a quick, defiant glance from under her fake eyelashes. Lipstick was smeared on her lips. She left the room without saying a word.

"Now, ladies. I presume you're Courtney's friend Layla, right?" DeShawn said.

I nodded. "Nice to meet you, DeShawn."

"Nice rack, Layla. Fake tits would be better, but this natural shit isn't bad at all."

"Um, thanks."

"You lookin' for a job as a stripper only or a hooker, too?"

"Just a stripper."

"What a fuckin' shame. I bet you can do fuckin' miracles with this pink pussy of yours." He glanced between my legs. He ogled me like a rapist.

"Layla has experience in the industry, but not among this clientele," Courtney said.

"You were a hooker?" he asked.

I clenched my fist and relaxed it. "An expensive call girl."

"Good luxurious pussy ain't bad. Get up and turn around."

I looked at Courtney. She nodded. I got up and spun around.

"Damn, girl. That's what I'm lookin' for right there. An ass to die for." He licked his lips.

"Thanks."

"Any experience with dancing?" he asked.

"Not much, but Courtney taught me some moves."

"Good. She'll teach you a couple more and you'll be good to go. We don't run a fuckin' dance school here. If you can shake your ass, your dancing skills are good enough."

DeShawn got up. I took a step back, but fortunately he didn't notice it. He walked to the desk, opened a drawer and pulled out a blunt. He lit it up, puffed and looked at me.

"You're hired, Layla. You'll start on Monday. Come here at eight. Courtney will tell you about the pay and all that shit."

"Thank you, DeShawn."

"Now go before I change my mind and decide to fuck you for a trial run."

My eyes went wide. Courtney shook her head.

DeShawn burst out laughing. "Just fuckin' with you, Layla. I don't fuck my best strippers. Only some of the hookers."

We left his office and walked in silence through the hallway and the main room. When we left the building and got into Courtney's car, she placed her hand on my shoulder.

"You did good, Olivia."

"Um... Thanks. Thanks for the introduction and the warning, too."

"DeShawn wants to prepare you for the clients. Believe me, what he said and did was mild compared to what happens in the club on a daily basis."

Chapter 3

MAX

I was a shitty private investigator. I hadn't even asked Victoria for her number. I had no other way of finding out who the black guy was before the office was open on Monday again, and I already had something else to do on Monday.

I tried the phone number I called a few weeks ago when Olivia showed up on my doorstep as an escort, but the woman who answered it refused to help me. There was nothing else to do on this day, so I called Tim to put into motion Olivia's plan.

"How are you doing, man?" I said.

"Busying myself with work," he said. He sounded apathetic and broken. There was nothing in his voice that reminded me of the old Tim, a person who had never been sad.

"Find some time tomorrow. I'm taking you somewhere."

"I'm not really in the mood to get out, Max."

"Trust me, it will be fun. This time it's you who can't say no."

He sighed. "Okay. But if you're taking me to a cheery place, I'll strangle you."

"Chill out. It will be fun. I'm not taking you to a circus."

"Okay. I trust you. See you tomorrow, then."

***

"Laser tag arena? Are you fucking kidding me?" Tim said.

"Relax, man. It will be fun, I promise."

We went inside and got our guns. The clerk sent me a wink. I excused myself for a second and texted Olivia.

"We're here. Ready?"

Her reply came seconds later.

"Just left her inside. Get Tim."

I slid the phone in my pocket and looked up. Tim looked so silly with a laser gun in his hand and a scowl on his face that I had to resist a chuckle. He reminded me of a kid angry at his parents because they didn't let him play outside.

"Everything okay?" he asked.

"Yeah. Just needed to send a quick text. You ready?"

"I don't think I'll ever get more ready for this shit. I don't see it fixing my mood."

"It will. Trust me. Come on."

I guided him through the long, darkly-lit corridor that reminded me of a post-apocalyptic shelter. Just as we were about to turn left and enter the hallway leading into the main arena, the door to the women's bathroom closed. I noticed a strand of blond hair disappearing inside. Tim was oblivious to what was about to happen.

"Come on, man," I said. "Ladies first."

"Fuck you," he said in a slightly amused tone. If everything went right, he shouldn't strangle me after leaving the room.

We entered a large, dark arena lit up with green, red and blue lights. The place reminded me of a huge labyrinth. It would give an epileptic a seizure, a claustrophobic an anxiety attack and a guy on acid the weirdest trip of his life.

"Hey, man. I need to take a piss," I said. "Your flag is in the base at the right. Be back in a sec."

I left the arena. Olivia waited for me at the entrance. She was dressed in sexy tight jeans and a simple black top that emphasized her round breasts. Her straight blond hair flew past her shoulders. She was so beautiful.

She pulled out a padlock from her pocket and locked the entrance.

I smiled at her. "And now we wait."

"I hope it won't take several days."

I laughed. "I hope not."

She sent me a weak smile and sat cross-legged against the metal door. A loose strand of hair fell over her cheek. I crouched beside her and brushed it aside. She closed her eyes and took in a long breath.

"The fact you helped me here doesn't mean I trust you again, Max. I need time. Or better yet, proof."

"I'm working on it."

"Real proof, Max. I need to hear the truth from the person who did it, if it really wasn't you."

A twinge of anger shot through my body. Then I looked in her beautiful blue eyes and calmed myself down. "I'll deliver you the proof you want, Olivia. I'm sorry you don't trust me, but I guess my comments didn't exactly give you a reason to."

She hid her face between her hands and moved her fingers through her hair. "I'm sorry."

Someone pushed on the handle. "Olivia?" Courtney said.

"Courtney?" I heard Tim's muffled voice.

"What the hell are you doing here?" she asked.

"And what the hell are you?"

"The door is locked," Courtney said. "Olivia," she yelled.

"I'm here," Olivia said. "Along with Max. We're not going to let you out until you settle the things between you. With guns or words, I don't care."

I resisted a chuckle. I felt like a father settling a fight between his kids.

A father. I had never wanted kids, but when I met Olivia, I realized I wouldn't mind starting a family with her. Hopefully my plan would work out and I would find the proof Olivia wanted to trust me again.

"I hate you, you bitch," Courtney yelled.

"You motherfucking cocksucker. Let us out," Tim growled.

I burst out laughing. With Olivia by my side, whether she was pissed at me or not, my life was so much better. Even if my best friend just called me a cocksucker.

"This is not funny, Max. Let us out," Courtney said in a pleading voice.

"Not going to happen, darling. Play a round or two with Tim and maybe you'll get tired enough to sit down and talk with each other," Olivia said.

"I can't believe you could do this to me, Olivia," Courtney said.

"We're going for a walk. We'll be back in an hour or two. Don't bother yelling for the clerk, she knows about everything," I said. "And I wouldn't call anyone else. It would be really awkward for you."

"You're dead, Max. I'll fucking kill you," Tim said.

"I doubt it, dude. If anything, you'll thank me."

I rose up and helped Olivia get up. The short moment I held her soft hand was enough to send a jolt of electricity through my body.

We walked down the hallway and stopped at the reception desk. The clerk looked up at us.

"Are they sorting it out?" she asked.

"Something along those lines. We'll be back in an hour or two. I'm sure they'll leave the arena happy," I said.

"Thank you for doing this, Patricia," Olivia said.

"My pleasure. I hate when people can't communicate. It fucks up a relationship."

I glanced at Olivia. She gazed at me with guilt written all over her face.

"Let's go, Olivia. I know a small cool park around here."

"All right."

I led her to my Mercedes. If everything turned out all right, I expected Tim to drive back with Courtney to her place or his. Then Olivia would be forced to call a cab or let me drive her home.

"I saw how you looked at me when she said it," Olivia said as I pulled onto the street and turned right. The park was a couple minutes away by car.

"And I saw how you looked at me. I'm hurt that you don't trust me, but I'll get the proof and we'll fix everything. I'm sure of it."

Olivia looked through the window. Her phone buzzed. She glanced at the screen and pressed her lips together. Whoever was calling, she didn't feel comfortable picking up the phone in my presence. Then she clicked on the screen and brought the phone to her face.

"Hey, Jamal. How are you doing?"

It sounded as if she had adjusted the volume of the speaker, because all I could hear was a couple muffled words. I was pretty sure I heard the word 'escort.'

"No. There were some… consequences. I'll be working at Black Cat now."

Black Cat. The name reminded me of something, but I couldn't remember what. I hoped it wasn't a brothel.

"Yeah. Victoria fired me. Thanks to her, I'm not going to work in the industry anymore."

I turned left and strained my ears. Whoever called her, it sounded as if he was her close colleague.

"How's business with your brother?"

More muffled words.

"Good for you. And yes, I heard about it. It's terrible."

I was pretty sure I heard the male voice say something about changing a career.

"It's just a temporary thing, Jamal. I don't really like him, but I have no other choice."

I stopped at the intersection. The park was just around the corner, a minute or so away.

"Yeah. Starting today. Courtney will take care of me."

Fuck. I remembered what Black Cat was. A seedy strip club and a brothel in one of the worst neighborhoods in town. It meant Courtney had been working there, but Courtney wasn't like Olivia. She had the rough edge Olivia didn't possess. People who visited cheap night clubs were different from the people who ordered expensive call girls. What the fuck was she getting herself into?

"Don't worry, I'll handle myself. How's your family?" Olivia said to the phone.

I turned right. The park was in sight. I pulled into the parking lot and turned the engine off.

"You too. We definitely need to catch up. I'll call you later."

I got out of the car and locked it when Olivia appeared on the other side.

She hung up and walked around the car. "Sorry," she said.

"No worries."

We walked down the pavement. A couple palm trees, shrubs and some dry grass grew on both sides of the trail.

"Care to elaborate about this job at Black Cat?" I asked.

"It's not really your issue, Max."

"Please. Don't cut me out, even if you're still angry at me."

"I'll be working with Courtney as a stripper. No private lap dances, just pole dancing."

I sighed. "You know I can borrow you some money until you find a better job?"

"I don't accept charity, Max. Never have, never will."

"Fine."

I sat on the bench under a leafy tree that gave some shade. Olivia sat beside me.

"And please don't mess this up. Don't go there threatening to kill somebody if I keep working as a stripper," she said.

"I won't. It's not my call to tell you where to work. You're a big girl capable of making her own choices."

Olivia scanned my face. Her hand slowly went up. She cupped my cheek and gave me a peck on the lips. I gazed deep in her eyes, unsure of what to do. She parted her lips. I pulled her in and slid my tongue in her mouth. She tasted even better than I remembered. No woman in the world had ever made me feel as good as Olivia, even if we only had an innocent kiss.

Okay, not so innocent. I penetrated her with my tongue as if I would die if we parted lips. My cock stiffened. I felt Olivia's nipples harden under her black top.

"Oh, God, I can't even begin to tell you how I missed it," I said.

"I'm so sorry, Max. I shouldn't have accused you. What you said a while ago… I saw it on your face. I was so stupid to believe it was you."

"It's okay, babe." I pulled her into my arms. "I'll find out the truth."

"It had to be another escort. They will get more clients if I'm gone until they hire someone else."

"Don't think about it. Leave it to me. You should think about your career after this stripping gig."

"I think I'll have to work there for at least a couple months. Maybe then I'll come up with something new."

I had a feeling Olivia hadn't thought about alternatives, but I decided against pointing it out. I should have asked her about the Mercedes and the black man then, but I forgot about it.

One hour later, we were back at the laser tag arena. We tiptoed to the door. The unmistakable sound of people having sex came from inside. I turned my head to Olivia and smiled. There were few things in the world that felt better than fixing someone's relationship.

I grabbed Olivia's hand and led her to the bathroom. Not romantic, I know, but given our history, it only felt fitting to have our reunion sex at the sink again.

I locked the door and pinned her against the tiles beside the sink. I pressed my lips against hers and slid my tongue inside. My cock brushed against Olivia's center. I wondered whether my dick could make a hole in my jeans. I was so rock-hard I could barely think straight.

Olivia let out a light moan and rubbed herself against me. I let one of her hands free and reached under her top. I unclasped her bra and hiked her shirt above her tits.

I lowered my head and flicked the tip of my tongue over her pink bud. Olivia squeezed my neck and pressed me against her. I wrapped my lips around her nipple and sucked it. Her sweet taste filled my mouth.

I let go of her other hand and squeezed her tits. My tongue glided around her swollen buds. I lifted my head and plunged my tongue deep into her mouth, savoring the sensation of her tongue dancing with mine. She cupped my cheeks and grinded her body against mine.

"Fuck me against the wall, Max. Now," she said in a begging, shaky voice.

If I had ever been close to coming by hearing someone's voice alone, it was at this moment.

I unbuttoned her jeans and slid them down. I removed her shoes and lay her pants underneath her feet. She wore my favorite black lace thong. It lay beside the jeans a second later. Olivia kneeled in front of me and unbuckled my pants. She slid them down to my ankles. My cock twitched under the fabric when her soft fingers brushed against it.

She slid her hand under the elastic band of my boxers. I panted when her fingers slowly glided across my hard length. Olivia licked my cock through the fabric while her hand moved up and down. I had never endured a worse torture.

"I need to taste you first," she said and slid my boxers down to my ankles. My cock brushed against her full lips while she did so. She blew hot air over my tip. I raked my fingers through her hair.

"What about fucking against the wall?" I said.

"Oh, you're so impatient," she said and swirled the tip of her wet tongue over my cockhead. I gasped and groaned. She gripped my root and parted her lips. God, few views were better than Olivia kneeling in front of me with her lips wrapped around my cock.

I growled and brushed my fingers against her sexy, soft cheek. She looked up. I once heard that you should fall in love with someone's eyes because it's the only thing that never changes. When I gazed at her perfect sky blue eyes, I had no doubt that they could only get more beautiful with time.

The fact that her lips were wrapped around my cockhead didn't hurt, either.

Olivia's eyes shone like sapphires when we had sex. When she looked at me from this vulnerable position, they were even more sparkling. Few things were a stronger turn-on than her mesmerizing fuck-me eyes.

As impossible as it sounds, my cock stiffened even more as her head moved up and down its length.

"I need to be inside you," I groaned. I helped her get up and pinned her against the wall. I pulled out a condom from my pocket and rolled it onto my cock.

Olivia lifted her right leg. I grabbed it with my hand and positioned my dick at her slick entrance. Then I buried my cock deep inside her. She whimpered and dug her fingers into my shoulders.

"Oh, yes," she moaned. "Deep and hard."

I withdrew and slipped back in. A burning hot sensation shot from my crotch. I wasn't going to last long with the sexy moans escaping her mouth right beside my ear.

"Wrap your legs around me," I said and lifted her.

Olivia interlocked her legs around my waist. I pushed my hips forward to increase the friction against her clit. Then I squeezed her ass and bounced her body on my cock. Groans and grunts filled the bathroom. Olivia slid her hands underneath my shirt and dug her nails in my back. I loved how she sometimes liked to mix pain with pleasure. I picked up the tempo. An orgasm built up inside me.

Olivia whimpered and her body tensed. I thrust deep inside her while rubbing the root of my shaft against her clit. She shook and cried out. I regretted I couldn't see her eyes in this moment. I loved to watch her face as she came.

Her hips trembled under my strong grip. I slid my cock in and out while she groaned and panted. My legs were exhausted. I slowed down my thrusts as her breath slowly evened out.

"I need to put you down," I said.

"Okay," she said in a dreamy, sultry voice.

I let her stand and pulled out. My legs burned just like after a session of squats at the gym.

"Good workout, huh?" she said with a smile on her face. Her bright blue eyes shone with excitement and relief at the same moment.

I laughed and brushed a strand of loose hair from her face. I loved her bright post-climax rosy cheeks. My phone buzzed.

"It must be Tim," I said.

"We haven't got you off yet," Olivia said and slid her hand against my sheathed cock. It stirred under her touch.

"It's fine. Let's get our friends before they get into a fight again."

"A couple minutes won't make a difference, baby." Olivia squeezed my cockhead and moved her hand up and down.

It was hard to argue with her.

Olivia placed her hands on the sink and tilted her ass. It was only then I noticed a mirror above the sink. She smiled at me. Her beautiful heart-shaped butt invited me to slip my cock inside her wet pussy and I could still see her lustrous eyes. It was so perfect.

I brushed the tip of my cock against her wet folds and thrust inside. A shot of red-hot pleasure darted through my body as I felt her warmth and tightness around my shaft.

"God. I won't last long," Olivia moaned.

I wasn't going to last long, either. I looked in the mirror. Her lips were parted and her eyes half-shut. I sunk inside her again and slowly picked up the pace. Olivia's moans didn't help me control myself. My cock pulsed inside her as I pounded her.

Her groans became louder and louder. Olivia slid her right hand between her legs and stroked her clit. Her face was twisted in ecstasy. When I saw her bite her lip and throw her head back I couldn't control myself any longer. I squeezed her ass and drove into her in a desperate rhythm.

I passed the point of no return. A tingling sensation enveloped my cock and lower stomach. I growled and yelled as I emptied myself into the condom. Olivia's walls squeezed my cock tighter.

She jerked her hips forward and let out a long, quiet moan. I glanced in the mirror. Her beautiful mouth was wide open, shaped in the perfect "O" I loved so much. I leaned my face onto her back and wrapped my arms around her waist. Beads of sweat trickled down my forehead.

"I love when you do that," Olivia said.

"Fuck you silly or lay my head on your back?"

She chuckled. "Both things."

I withdrew and tossed the condom in the wastebasket. Olivia reached for her crumpled jeans and panties. I put on my clothes. Then I unlocked my phone and read aloud the message from Tim.

"It's Tim," I said. "Come and get us, fucker. I still want to kill you, but maybe you'll get a pardon."

Olivia laughed. "It worked."

"I had no doubt it would work. You're a genius, Olivia."

"Flattery will get you everywhere." She batted her eyelashes.

"Let's get our friends. I hope they had as much fun as we did."

"I doubt anybody could have as much fun as we just did, honey," Olivia said.

Both she and I looked like people who'd just had sex, but I didn't care. Courtney and Tim probably wouldn't look much different.

We left the bathroom and walked to the metal door. Olivia pulled out the key to the padlock and unlocked it. Courtney sat on Tim's lap on a wooden crate. She had disheveled hair. Tim didn't look better in his crumpled shirt and pants.

"You two had fun?" Olivia said.

"I want to kill you and hug you at the same time," Courtney said. She got up and interlocked her fingers with Tim's. They sauntered over to us. When they saw our faces, they exchanged a glance and laughed. I squeezed Olivia's hand and we burst into laughter, too.

Two relationships saved with a trip to a laser tag arena. Not bad, eh?

Chapter 4

OLIVIA

Max and Tim exchanged their usual insults, questioning their sexual orientation while I hugged Courtney and told her how happy I was they got back together. Then Max drove me back home in his Mercedes while Courtney drove away with Tim in her red Micra.

It was a funny sight to see his handsome face looking through the window of one of the most girly cars in the world.

My phone buzzed on our way back to my place. It was a text from my aunt.

"Surgery scheduled for Wednesday."

I texted my reply. "I'll be there." I would piss off DeShawn for taking time off so soon, but I wanted to be there for my mom.

Thirty or so minutes later, Max and I were at my place. I still had a couple hours before I had to leave for my first evening at Black Cat, so I figured I had time for a quick reunion tea with my man. I turned the kettle on. My phone rang. I didn't recognize the number of the caller.

"Layla?" a familiar voice said. I couldn't pinpoint who it was exactly.

"Yes. Who's calling?"

"DeShawn."

"Oh, I'm sorry. I don't have your number in my contacts."

"And you don't have to. You're not goin' to work in my club."

A knot formed in my stomach. "Why? What's wrong?"

"I don't have time for fuckin' boyfriend drama."

I glanced at Max, who was playing with Luna in the hallway. "What?"

"Your boyfriend called me a couple minutes ago telling me he would call the cops on my place if I hired you. I don't have time to track him down and give him a good ass-whoopin', so I'm firing you instead."

"Wait. He called you when?"

"Have you lost your fuckin' hearing? I said he called a couple minutes ago."

I walked over to the fridge to hide from Max. "It wasn't my boyfriend. He's been with me for the past couple hours."

"I don't care who it was. I have enough drama in my club as it is. I don't need scenes with your boyfriend or whoever the fuck he was. Sort your shit out and then maybe I'll consider you again. Or maybe not. Definitely not."

"DeShawn…"

"Shut up. You're a nice piece of ass, but I need drama-free bitches. Good luck with whatever you're going to do now. Don't call me again or I'll take the trouble of finding your boyfriend."

He hung up. I clenched the phone in my hand and resisted the urge to toss it across the kitchen.

I had the proof that whoever was making my life difficult wasn't Max.

I don't think I had ever felt angrier at myself that I let my emotions take control over the logical part of my brain. All the drama with Max could have been avoided if I sat down, counted to ten and considered all other possible reasons for the situation at the office.

Then again, I had rarely used logic alone during my decision making process.

Max entered the kitchen and gazed at me. "Everything okay?"

"I'm so sorry, Max. I was so stupid to accuse you." I pulled him into my arms and leaned my head onto his shoulder. A tear trickled down my cheek. Max broke the embrace and looked into my eyes.

"Babe, what happened?" he said.

"DeShawn, the manager of Black Cat, just called me. Somebody called him pretending he was my boyfriend. The caller warned him he would call cops on him if he hired me."

"It wasn't me."

I felt a pang of guilt. "I know. He called a couple minutes ago, around the time we pulled into the driveway."

"Did he fire you?"

"I lost my chance to work there. He was pissed off. Who the fuck has anything to gain by making my life so difficult?"

Max stroked my face. The water started to boil, so I turned the kettle off.

"Sit down. Let's have some tea and think about it."

He guided me toward the table and shuffled the chair away from it. I plopped into the chair and rested my head on my hands. Max poured water into the mugs and put them on the table. He grabbed a chair and placed it beside mine.

"Let's think about it. Whoever called him must have known you were going to work there."

"Only Courtney and you know about it."

"I have a pretty good alibi. What about Courtney?"

"She didn't like the idea of me working there, but I've known her long enough to know she would never do it to me. Besides, it was a man who called DeShawn."

"Tim would never do it if Courtney asked him, so we can rule them out. Anybody else? One of the strippers who didn't like the prospect of another girl competing with her?"

"There was this… girl at DeShawn's office. He asked her to leave when… when we spoke with him. I'm pretty sure she didn't like me."

Max took a sip of tea and moved a hand through his hair. It was still tousled after our quickie in the bathroom. "What about the phone call?"

"What phone call?"

"You spoke with someone on our way to the park. You told him you were going to work at Black Cat with Courtney."

"It was Jamal, my ex-bodyguard. He's out of the business."

"Would he have a reason to hurt you?"

"He had cared for me since day one. Nobody at the agency cared for me more than Jamal."

Max's eyes went wide. "Wait. Is he a big black guy?"

"Yes. What does it—"

59

"Does he drive a black Mercedes?"

"Yes, he does. Or at least used to when he was my driver. Do you know him?"

"After our conversation at the café, I drove to the agency's office to speak with Victoria. There was this teenager who told me he saw a huge black guy in a black Mercedes late at night. The same night someone messed up the office."

"It doesn't make sense. Why would he do that?"

"I have no idea, but it wouldn't hurt to ask him, would it?"

I couldn't believe Jamal would do anything like this, but then again, I wrongly accused Max. I owed it to him to at least make the call.

"I'll call him," I said.

"Tell him to come here and catch up. Tell him I'll be here, too."

"Okay."

I reached for my phone and dialed Jamal's number. He picked up after the second ring.

"Hey, Olivia. What's up?" No way it could have been Jamal who did all of this. His voice was too calm and relaxed.

"I thought about our last conversation. I'm free this afternoon and evening. Wanna catch up? My boyfriend is here. I'd love you two to get to know each other."

"Sure. Of course."

"Five at my place?"

"I'll be there."

"See you."

I hung up and glanced at Max.

"He knew you had your first night at the club today. Why didn't he ask why you have a free evening?"

"Because he forgot about it?"

"We'll find out soon enough."

I wasn't sure if I was ready for the truth.

***

"Jamal, Max. Max, Jamal," I said. The guys shook hands and we all sat down in my living room. Jamal eyed Max with a suspicious gaze. I didn't

61

blame him. A couple weeks ago, he was ready to blow Max's head off after he saw me running down the street with tears trickling down my face.

"Do you want anything to drink?" I asked.

"Coffee would be perfect," Jamal said. "Black."

"Max?"

"Just a glass of water, babe."

Five minutes later, we sat together in the living room. Max sat at my left on the sofa while Jamal sat in front of us in the armchair.

"How's your business going, Jamal?" I asked.

"The business is good. I'm glad I'm no longer working for the agency, but I have to admit I miss our rides."

"Yeah, me too," I said. "Everything working out between you and your brother?"

"He's a business genius. We shipped more than a hundred items in the last two weeks, and we're only one month in."

"Good for you, Jamal. I'm happy to hear that."

Max stared at the glass of water in his hand.

There was awkward tension in the air. Luna defused it when she entered the living room and jumped on Jamal's lap.

"Where were you, Luna?" Jamal said.

"Probably warming herself up on the porch. Nothing like good nap in the sun after dinner," I said.

Max squeezed my hand. I gazed at him. He slightly jerked his chin toward Jamal.

"Jamal, I need to ask you something," I said.

He lifted his head and looked at me. "What's up?"

"Have you been at the office since you handed in your notice?"

Jamal glanced at Max and then at me.

"Yeah, I was there once or twice. I grabbed the shit I forgot to take before."

"Grab your shit?" Max said. "Or maybe made a fucking mess?"

"Max," I said and squeezed his hand. Jamal pursed his lips. His nostrils flared. Luna must have noticed his anger because she climbed onto his chest and brushed her tongue against his chin.

"Do you have anything to tell me, Jamal?" I asked.

"Like what?" he said.

"Dude, I know you were at the office the night someone messed it up. And I'm pretty sure you made a friendly call to the manager of Black Cat today," Max said.

"What's this all about, Layla?" Jamal said.

"Shouldn't you tell us about it?" Max said.

Jamal clenched his fists. If I didn't do something to ease the tension, they were going to kill each other in my bedroom.

"I just want to know the truth, Jamal. Was it you who left the warning at the office and called DeShawn today?" I said.

"Did you hear about the escort killing a couple weeks ago?"

"I did."

"What about this girl who was beaten into a coma?"

"I heard about that, too."

"I knew both of them. The first one, Alicia, worked for the agency a couple years ago. You remind me of her. Just like her, you're trying to fit yourself in a job that doesn't suit you."

"So was it you?"

"And the second girl, the one in a coma? She worked for the agency for a couple weeks before I got reassigned to you and she went on her own. A troublemaker, that one, but she didn't deserve a beating. Her client was on coke."

"Did you—"

"I did all of this to protect you. I failed to protect Alicia, and I failed Delilah. I'm not going to let the same happen to you."

"Jamal…"

"Let him speak," Max said.

"After this bald fucker almost killed you, I knew it was my last chance to protect you. That's why I left the agency, hoping that you wouldn't like to return if you had to work with another guy. It didn't work, so I had to come up with something else. I knew that talking with you wouldn't do shit."

I wanted to strangle him. At the same time, I wanted to hug him. He had a selfless motivation. As much as it complicated my life, he did it because I was important to him.

"Why did you scare away DeShawn?"

"His place is a hellhole. DeShawn is decent for a pimp and club manager, but his employees and clients are not. Ask Courtney about Harmony or Ivy. The same thing would happen to you."

"What thing?"

"Beaten, raped, killed? Pick your poison. All of this shit goes down in Black Cat."

Max gazed at me with pursed lips. Great, two guys who wanted to kill each other a second ago now formed a front against me.

"What the fuck do you want me to do? Let go of all my dreams and become a fucking housewife?"

"A safer job would be a good start," Jamal said. "Neither escort services nor stripping is a good career choice for you. I've been in both industries for long enough to know how they treat the women who work in them."

"Jamal is right. Courtney is a tough girl. I'm pretty sure she would beat me and Jamal bloody if we startled her in a dark alley. You're not like her," Max said.

"Then who am I? Come on, tell me. You two know me so fucking well you might as well be my shrinks."

"I remember how you told me you'd like to work in the tourism industry," Jamal said. "Why not start there? I can refer you to some people."

"I need money right now. I can't live on peanuts."

"I can help you," Max said. "There's no need for you to go back into the industry. Get out, just like me, and let's build something new together."

"We can help you, Layla," Jamal said. "We care about you, and we only want the best for you. The sex industry ain't it."

I saw red. These men had no right to tell me what to do with my life, motivated by their care for me or not. "Get out, both of you."

"Babe, what's wrong?" Max said.

"Get out. I want to be alone."

Jamal exchanged a glance with Max, put Luna on the sofa and stood up. Max glared at me and followed Jamal. They left my house without saying a word.

I felt guilty for being so brusque, but what was I supposed to do? I couldn't listen to their arguments any longer. I was a grown woman. I was capable of making my own choices. Max acted as if he had understood it, but then he joined Jamal in coaxing me to rethink my choices.

I was burned as an escort and as a stripper. There was only one choice left. I would regret it, but I wasn't about to give in and start a boring, dead end job only because it was less risky than the industry in which I worked. I reached for my phone and dialed the number.

"Hey, Fiona. Do you still work with Larry?"

"Yeah, honey. How can I help you?"

"Set up a meet with him. I need a new job."

Next stop: Montpelier, Vermont. I had to get away from it all. Alone.

Chapter 5

MAX

"Can you make any sense of it?" I asked Jamal as we walked down the driveway of Olivia's house.

"No fucking idea. We just wanna help, and that's what we get in return."

"Olivia has been pretty rattled recently. The beating, job loss, another job loss."

"I never learned her real name. It's pretty. Suits her better than Layla."

"Sure it does."

We stopped beside my car. I smiled when I saw Jamal's black Mercedes.

"A Mercedes fan, huh?" I said.

"Nobody builds better cars, dude. I'd love to get my hands on an old W115, but I'd rather invest money in my new business."

"W115 was a beauty, dude. I wouldn't mind driving one, either. What industry are you in?"

"Home alarms and other security stuff. E-commerce."

"Good for you, man." I patted him on the back.

Just fifteen minutes ago, I wanted to kill this man for messing up my relationship with Olivia. Now, I decided I liked him. There was no doubt he knew some seedy elements and could take care of himself in case some serious shit went down. At the same time, there was a casual aura around him – no bullshit, just getting things done.

"What about you, man? What are you doing now that you're no longer an escort?" he asked.

I glanced at the door of Olivia's house and gazed at Jamal. "Hey man, why don't we grab a beer or two? I know a cool pub not far away from here. I want to pick your mind about something."

"Sure. I'll follow you."

Twenty minutes later, we sat in The Lamb with mugs of beer on the table. I reminded myself to limit my alcohol intake to one mug only. The Lamb's parking lot wasn't the best place to leave the car overnight, especially if you drove a Mercedes.

"So, what's your new job?" Jamal asked.

"I'm sort of in-between. I no longer work as an escort. I started coaching a couple guys about the industry."

"How does it look? You teach them to lick pussy and shit like that?"

I laughed. Jamal followed me. His hearty laugh made me like him even more.

"Among other things, yeah. I teach them how to dress, how to seduce, how to take care of the paperwork and other stuff. Obviously it's not as lucrative as providing the services myself, but after I met Olivia, I couldn't do it any longer."

"She's not just a random girl for you, is she?"

"Definitely not. I have plans for her."

"What plans?"

I glanced at him and considered whether I should trust him.

"Just a friendly question, man," Jamal said. "Olivia has been almost like my daughter while my family was away."

"Has she ever told you what she would do if money was not an issue?"

"Yeah, I remember. She would start her own small beachfront hotel and get her Mom to help her."

"That's pretty much what she told me, too. Now, I know that her house is paid off. I have a lot of savings, plus I own my house, too. All I lack is a property to turn into a hotel."

Jamal raised his eyebrows and exhaled. "Man, you're really serious about her."

"She suspected it was me who messed up the office because I talked with her and told her I would find another way to get her out of the industry."

"I'm so sorry for this, dude. I didn't know it would land on you."

"Let's focus on what we have now, Jamal. I was in Mexico with her for a few days a couple weeks ago. She loved all the places I showed here there."

"What state? Quintana Roo?"

"Yeah. South of Playa del Carmen."

"No shit. Dude, it's my favorite part of Mexico."

"Do you travel there often?"

"I worked there for a year in my early twenties. I still visit it at least once a year."

"Do you still have contacts there?"

Jamal nodded. "I can make some calls."

"Anyone working in the real estate industry or someone looking to sell a beachfront property?"

"I can ask around. I should be able to come up with something."

I can't even begin to tell you how happy I was to hear it. I wanted to get up and hug the man, even though I was pretty sure he would crush me with his huge arms.

***

"What the fuck are you doing?" I asked.

"Licking her pussy," he said.

"Where the fuck did you learn that? In a fucking porno? Man, this is real life. Use the entire surface of your tongue."

Chad had been one sexy motherfucker even for me – a heterosexual man – but sometimes he was so clueless about how to make love to a woman I wondered if he really had clients.

I brought the unused artificial pussy to my mouth and pressed the flat of my tongue against the bottom of it. I slowly licked its entire length. Thanks to a thorough washing, it only smelled and tasted of soap.

"That's how you do it."

Chad nodded.

"Flick your tongue from time to time, but not the entire time. Most women find it annoying as fuck."

"Okay, will do."

If someone walked in on us while I was giving him sex education lessons, it would be a flabbergasting experience for her. We looked like a couple of psychos.

"How are things with Charlotte? Still squeezing your face between her legs?"

Chad scowled. "Yeah."

I laughed. This woman would never change. I was glad I was out of the business. Coaching young escorts didn't pay as much, but it was still made me money.

My phone rang. "Sorry, man."

"No problem," he said and leaned his face onto the artificial pussy.

I left my living room and went to the kitchen. I glanced at the screen of my phone. It was Olivia. Finally. I hadn't heard from her since Monday. I started to get worried.

"Hey, Max."

"Hey, babe. Everything okay?"

"I'm sorry for Monday. I had to be alone for a while."

"No problem. I get it. You at home now?"

"No, I'm in Vermont."

"Vermont? Did something happen to your mom?"

"She's... she's having a surgery right now."

"What happened?"

"That's why I can't start working at a regular job. I paid for a new treatment for her arthritis. She shouldn't need her meds any longer, but I'm close to declaring bankruptcy."

"I can—"

"No. I'll manage. I don't want to cut you out again, Max, but please don't talk about my job. Let me do my thing. If I need your help, I'll ask you for it."

"Okay."

"I'm just calling to check in and tell you what's going on with me. I should be back early next week for a job appointment."

"What j—," I bit my tongue. "Okay. What about Luna?"

"Courtney takes care of her, as always. If you want to say hi, Courtney has my permission to give you the keys."

"Thanks. I'll definitely check on my favorite cat in the world, but what I really crave is your pussy."

Olivia purred. Fuck, had there been a sexier sound than her purring and moans?

"I can't wait to ride your hard cock and take it in my mouth," she said.

"You should stop before I pack my shit and fly there."

"Just imagine me on my knees in front of you…"

"Seriously, I'm going to call a cab in a second. Just need to get Chad out of here."

"Who's Chad?"

I slapped my forehead. I forgot to tell her. "I have this new gig. I teach other guys how to be good escorts. I'm sorry I didn't tell you about it."

"Does it involve fucking them in the ass?" Olivia chuckled.

"You're disgusting."

"Just wondering."

"You better wonder what I'll do to you when you're back."

I heard a female voice in the background.

"I will, darling. I have to go now."

"Sure. Call me after the surgery, okay?"

"Okay."

I slid my phone back in my pocket and walked to my living room. Chad had been making progress with his tongue.

"Good. Once she's nice and wet and rubs her hips against you, focus on the clit."

"What about my fingers?"

"Slide one finger in at first, and add a second one later when she's ready. Listen to her breath to find out if she's into it. Some women prefer the tongue only, other won't come without fingering."

Chad slid his two fingers inside the artificial pussy and lapped at it with his tongue.

I laughed. Talking about pussy all day long had never been so fun.

Chapter 6

OLIVIA

I didn't believe in God, but I guess my obsessive thoughts during Mom's surgery could count as praying. The phone call with Max helped me relieve some of the tension, but when my aunt interrupted our conversation, I was a bundle of nerves again.

I hung up and gazed at Auntie. She jerked her chin toward the hallway. The surgeon, a forty-something brunet with cleanly shaved cheeks and thick eyebrows walked in our direction.

"Good news, ladies. The surgery went well. We expect a full recovery. She would still have limited ability to use her hands for another two weeks or so. After that, she should feel as if she had a new set of hands."

"Oh my God, thank you so much," I said. "Can we see her?"

"Not yet. The nurse will call you later."

"Thank you so much, Doc," Auntie said.

"Just doing my job." He put a hand on my shoulder and left me and Auntie alone in the waiting room. I pulled my aunt into my arms.

"You're the best daughter ever, Olivia."

"Just doing my job, Auntie."

We embraced each other and shared the laughter of joy.

Two days later Mom was back at home recuperating from the surgery. I sat on the porch of her old house on the outskirts of town and read a book on my Kindle. My phone buzzed. A shiver crept down my spine when I noticed it was a text from Fiona. I needed this job, but it freaked me out to think about it, nonetheless.

"Larry can see you on Wednesday afternoon. Does it work for you?"

I texted my reply. "Sure. What time?"

Her reply came seconds later. "1 PM."

"I'll be there," I replied.

After the costs of the flight, I had money to support myself for a little over a month. Larry's studio was the last place I wanted to visit, but at this point I couldn't afford waiting for any other option.

Porn business, here I come.

***

I woke up on Wednesday morning tired after the flight the day before. I was also stressed out. But then again, should I jump out of bed with joy at the prospect of a job interview with Larry, the King of Porn?

He paid good money, but he demanded a lot, too. If I was lucky, I could star in some vanilla lesbian movies. Working with men in hardcore porn, as lucrative as it could be, was the last thing on my list.

When I thought about Max and how hurt he would be after I told him where I worked, I decided against even considering the option. If I couldn't get a job in vanilla stuff, alone or with another girl, I would get a regular job for peanuts.

Me, a woman who vowed to never work in a cubicle. The world was coming to an end.

I stroked Luna's side and got out of bed. Three hours later, I sat in a cab taking me straight to Larry's studio. I don't think the driver had any doubts about why I was going there. I wore my sluttiest tight red mini skirt and a top with a lot of cleavage.

Larry's studio was located in a warehouse building in the industrial part of town. If you didn't know where to look for it, you would never find it. The long, gray building housed expensive studio equipment, rows of slutty clothes and lingerie, tons of lube and sex toys stacked on shelves. There were ten or so various scenes ready for filming – an office with expensive furniture, a doctor's office complete with fake medical equipment, a regular bedroom for vanilla productions and a small classroom, among others.

The set that bothered me the most was the dungeon for BDSM productions. I liked rough sex as much as the next woman, but I had no idea what people found appealing in hurting others. Well, to each his own, as they say.

I walked through the large main room behind a tall security guard who led me to Larry's office. We passed half-naked women, men casually stroking their cocks as if it was no big deal to do it in public and several guys wearing black t-shirts with "director" written on the back.

One naked redhead with fake tits jogged past me. Tears trickled down her face.

I didn't like this place at all.

The guard stopped by a small office at the west end of the building. He knocked on the door and disappeared inside.

A half-naked blond guy who looked like a teenager walked past me. "Hey," he said.

"Hey."

"You in for an interview?"

"Yeah."

"I hope Larry likes you. I'm looking forward to working with you."

The hungry way he looked at my rack made me uncomfortable. I sent him a fake smile. What the fuck was I doing? How could I do this to Max? I wanted to turn on my heels and go home when the door to the office opened and the guard motioned me to get inside.

"C'mon in, Layla," Larry said.

I only spoke with him once before I started working as an escort. Working in the porn industry was my first choice before an opportunity to work as an expensive call girl appeared on my radar.

Larry still wore big round black glasses and a full beard that made him look more like a librarian than the owner of a porn empire. He wore a white dress shirt and black pants. Just like over two years ago, his office was cluttered with stacks of papers and his walls decorated (if you could call it that) with pornographic posters.

The guard left the office and closed the door behind me.

"Please have a seat, Layla," Larry said and motioned with his hand toward a leather chair in front of his desk.

I walked over to the chair and sat down, thinking how many people had been fucked on it. I realized that thinking about working in the porn industry was different than actually sitting in the office of a porn king. I wanted to run away as soon as possible.

"Fiona told me you're looking for a job again."

"Yeah, I am."

"I checked your folder. I really liked what I saw there. If nothing had changed during the past two years, I'm willing to hire you."

My folder? Everything should have been destroyed the moment I made a call telling Larry I wasn't going to work for him. I decided against getting angry at him. As polite as he could be, Larry could get aggressive in an instant.

"I'm looking for a role in a lesbian movie. Or solo. No male-female stuff."

He leaned forward. His leather chair squeaked under his big frame. "I'm paying more for hardcore porn, Layla. Much more."

"I know, but it's not my thing."

"Your folder says you're heterosexual. Something changed?"

I considered my reply. "Your folder is outdated."

"That's a shame then. I have a great team for lesbian and solo stuff now, but I'm always looking for new hardcore actresses."

My phone buzzed. "I'm sorry, I'm waiting for an important call. Family stuff," I said.

"Sure, I'll go check on my girls."

Larry left the office. I pulled my phone from my handbag. It was a text from Max.

"Hey, honey. You back in town? Wanna meet in the evening and update me on your mom?"

A pang of guilt hit me like a shovel across the head. I was a terrible person for not sharing with him where I wanted to work.

"8 PM at my place?"

His reply came seconds later.

"Be there. P.S. Can't wait to taste you."

Larry walked back into the office as I was hiding my phone.

"Family stuff sorted out?"

"Yeah," I said.

"Then let's get to business," he said and brushed his hand against my bare shoulder. I shuddered at his touch. "Wow, you're so jumpy. That's not good in this business, sweetheart."

"You just startled me. I want to—"

"We'll talk about your pay and other stuff later, okay? First I want to take a couple new nude pictures, check how your body's shaping up now."

My throat was dry. "Larry, with all due respect, I don't think I'm a good fit for this job."

"Let me be the judge, Layla." He slid his hand under my top and squeezed my breasts.

It took all I had not to slap him in the face. When I was still close with Fiona, I heard a couple stories about how nasty Larry could get when he was angry.

I rose up. "I'm sorry, Larry. This job is not for me. Can I get my folder back?"

He cocked his brow. "Your folder? I own it, darling."

"I'd like to get it back. It was a mistake to come here. I'm not going to work in the porn industry."

"When you were here for your interview two years ago, you signed an agreement. I can show you the copy. You waived the rights to your nude pictures. Technically speaking, I could publish them on my sites and you couldn't do shit."

"What do you want, Larry?"

"I can't give it back to you, Layla. I never destroy the folders."

"How much do you want?"

"Honey, these are not for sale."

"Five hundred?"

Larry laughed. "I make more than that in an hour, Layla."

"One thousand."

"It's not for sale, Layla. I don't need your money."

"Two thousand five hundred."

It was close to all I had left in my bank account.

"Sorry, Layla."

I clenched my fists and took in a long breath.

"Fine," I said. "Thank you for the interview."

I walked over to the door and turned the knob.

"Layla?"

I turned around. "Yeah?"

"I like your style." Larry handed me the folder. "Take it."

I slid the folder in my handbag.

"Why are you doing this?" I asked.

"Just feeling like doing some good today."

I eyed his expression.

"I don't have any copies, Layla. Believe it or not, I like you. You could have threatened me with Fiona, but you didn't. I admire that."

Fiona was my old friend and Larry's best actress.

"Thank you."

"You better burn it before your kids or boyfriend see it."

"I will. Thank you, Larry."

"You should thank Fiona. If she found out I didn't give you back the folder, she would cut my cock."

I laughed. "Yeah, she would. Thanks again, Larry."

I left his office elated. It doesn't happen every day that you avoid making a huge mistake and fix a mistake you made two years ago.

My phone rang again when I left the studio. This time it was the call I had been waiting for.

"Hi, Mom. How was the visit?"

"Everything went great. The doctor said I'm recovering faster than a teenager."

The news made me so happy I forgot what I carried in my handbag.

Chapter 7

MAX

I hadn't seen Olivia for over a week, but it felt more like an eternity. When I finally knocked on her door and saw her standing on the doorstep, I pinned her against the wall and buried my tongue in her mouth like a starving dog. Fuck, I could taste her mouth for hours, if it wasn't for my cock painfully pressing against my boxers.

"Someone's happy to see me," Olivia whispered into my ear.

I slipped my hand inside her panties and brushed my finger against her wet folds. "Someone's happy about seeing me, too."

Something brushed against my leg. I looked down. Luna purred and rubbed her side against my calf.

"She's happy, too," Olivia chuckled.

"Cockblocked by a cat. Seriously?"

Olivia burst out laughing. Few things were sweeter to my ears than her laugh. Today, it was even more beautiful and carefree. She had good reasons to be happy. Her mom would get better, and she had a job interview that probably went well.

"How's your job interview?" I asked.

She pressed her lips together and relaxed them. A faint smile appeared on her face. "Good. I mean, I won't get it, but it wasn't for me, anyway."

"Care to elaborate?"

"Not today, Max. I just want to enjoy the evening, okay?"

"Sure."

I had to talk to her about it later. Something was off in her smile.

"Did you speak with Jamal or are you still angry at him?" I asked.

"You two hit it off, didn't you?"

"Yeah, he's a cool guy. I don't blame him for doing what he did. Do you?"

"It's okay between us. I spoke with him and we explained everything to each other."

"Are you going back to work for the agency?"

"No. You were right about it. It's not for me. And neither is the strip club."

I breathed a sigh of relief. "I'm happy to hear that."

"I can see," Olivia said and glided her hand over my crotch.

"Hey, bad girl. Don't tease me."

"Or what?"

"Or," I said and squeezed her ass, "I will take off your jeans and punish you."

"Oh, you're so scary, Max. I don't want your punishment." She leaned her face into mine and licked my earlobe.

I grabbed her neck and pulled her in. I nibbled her skin right under the ear and slid my tongue over her throat. "You shouldn't tease me while my teeth are so close to your throat, babe."

"Or what? You're going to suck my blood?"

I swirled my tongue over her collarbone. "I'll start with sucking your nipples." I hiked up her white top and licked her stomach. "And then I'll glide my tongue over your clit."

I unbuttoned her jeans and brushed my fingers against her smooth lower stomach. "And if you're a nice girl, I'll stay there for a while longer."

It always made me crazy to touch her soft skin right above her pussy, especially when she wore her sexy black lace panties. Add in her quiet panting, and my cock wanted to burn a hole through my pants.

"Sounds like a good plan," she whispered.

I grabbed her hips and carried her to the kitchen. I closed the door behind us. As much as I loved Luna, I didn't enjoy having sex in front of a cat.

OLIVIA

No man had ever made me wetter than Max. My day, which started out so bad, got better and better with each passing minute. When Max laid me down on the table and slid off my jeans, my day was about to turn into heaven on Earth. Then again, every day spent with him was like heaven on Earth.

I propped myself on my arms and reached out with my hands to Max's light blue dress shirt. He smiled at me and stroked my hair. I loved how well-dressed he had always been. I unbuttoned his shirt and hung it over the chair. He laid my body back on the table and towered above me, standing half-naked in sexy, dark pants.

God, even though I saw a fair share of naked men in my life, none of them could compare to Max. His muscular chest and rippled stomach were perfect – not overly bulky, and not so dry that he looked like a starved bodybuilder. I loved his chest hair that accentuated his manly build and complemented his light stubble.

"I missed you so much," I said.

"I can't even begin to tell you how much I missed you, Olivia."

He took off my white top and unclasped my bra. He cupped my breasts and took my nipple in his mouth. I threw my head back and panted. My nipples had always been sensitive, but they were even more susceptible to Max's touch. He had a gift in his hands.

No, I take it back – he had a gift in his large, hard hands, his full fleshy lips, and his cock that had always been so hard in my presence.

I couldn't exist without this man, plain and simple.

"Your nipples are so hard and sweet," he said.

"I love how you suck them." I ran my fingers through his thick black hair and slid my hand across his round, strong shoulders.

Max left a trail of wet kisses over my breasts and stomach. He blew hot air over my panties and slid his tongue across my thigh. I panted when his cheek slightly brushed against my hot crotch.

He kissed my leg and swirled his tongue over my kneecap. Max had enjoyed exploring unusual spots on my body. Before I had sex with him, I didn't even know that several parts of my body could feel so good when licked or massaged.

He grabbed my foot and rubbed it. Tension drifted away from my body like magic. Max massaged my other foot and kissed my other leg, leaving kisses and light bites from my ankle up to my inner thigh. His cheek once again brushed against the fabric of my panties. I gasped.

"Someone here is getting impatient," Max said.

"Oh, who could that be?" I whispered.

He pulled my panties to the side and pressed the flat of his tongue against my outer lips. He slowly slid it up and paused for a second right beside my throbbing clit.

"I'm not sure. Maybe it's you?" He turned his head to the side and glided his tongue over my clit.

I drew in a sharp breath. God, was there anything better than his tongue over my clit? Oh, right, there was. His cock inside me. But his tongue almost shared first place with his cock. Max didn't just slide his tongue over my pussy. He knew how to use his lips and bring pleasure in combination with his fingers.

He pulled my panties back over my wet pussy and leaned his face onto my breasts. He took my engorged nipple in his mouth and sucked it. His hand hovered over the fabric of my panties. The faint sensation of his fingertips brushing against my clit sent a pleasant, tingling feeling up my body. If he kept doing it, it wouldn't be the first time with him that I came while still wearing my panties.

Max licked my collarbone and bit my neck. I threw my head to the side. My neck had always been sensitive, and each light bite felt like a small explosion that spread pleasure over my entire body.

I grabbed his neck and brought him to my lips. He slid his tongue over my teeth and explored my mouth. His hard erection pressed through the fabric against my wet center. If I wanted to have one superpower, it would be the ability to make clothes disappear with a single thought. I wanted him inside me so badly I started rubbing my hips against his.

"Take them off and fuck me," I whispered into his ear.

"You're so impatient today, honey."

"And you're so cruel."

"Let me show you how cruel I can get."

Max shuffled a chair beside the edge of the table and pulled down my panties. He leaned his face between my legs and slowly licked my pussy, teasing my clit with light flicks. He squeezed my thighs and pinched my nipples. He flattened his tongue and glided it over the entire length of my pussy.

"I can't get enough of your taste," he said.

I moaned in response as his tongue slid over my pulsing clit. A fire blazed through my body, pushing me closer and closer to the verge of a climax. Max established a steady, slow rhythm with his tongue. Each time his tongue slid over my clit, he followed it with his full lips brushing against my most sensitive spot.

Max slid two fingers inside me and pressed them against my spongy G-spot. He made small circles over it. He focused his tongue on my clit, licking around it and across it. I groaned and gasped. A pleasurable ache spread from my core up to my stomach. My muscles tightened. I wriggled as Max kept me pinned against the table and pleasured me with his mouth.

"It feels so good, Max," I moaned. "I don't know if I want to come just yet."

"Just tell me what you want, baby." He stroked my G-spot with a come hither motion, sending surges of red-hot pleasure over my body. It rendered me breathless and wordless.

"Max," I cried out. "I…"

I drew in a sharp breath and jerked on the table. My body went into powerful spasms that flooded me with relief and blazing hot ecstasy that wiped out every thought from my mind.

His fingers and mouth kept stimulating my pussy and sent me soaring even higher. I drifted some several thousand miles above Earth, bathing in the most pleasant sensation in the universe.

After what seemed like an hour, the sensations slowly weakened and brought me back to my kitchen in Phoenix, AZ.

Max smiled at me with dreamy eyes. "I love to watch you when you're coming. I hope you're not angry I didn't stop."

"I was about to tell you to keep going."

"Glad we understood each other." Max chuckled.

I extended my hand. Max helped me sit on the edge of the table. I reached to his pants and unbuckled them. They were on the floor a couple seconds later, his hard cock pressed against the black fabric of his manly, tight boxer shorts. I brushed my hand against it. God, he was so hard that I found myself craving another orgasm a mere minute or so after the previous one.

"Take me on the table, Max," I said and slid down his boxers. His cockhead was wet with pre-cum. He stepped out of his boxers and stood naked and hard in front of me. I starved for his hardness inside me. Once I let a man like Max in my life, I couldn't go on longer than a couple days without getting intimate with him.

He positioned his cock at my wet center and dragged it down the length of my slick entrance.

"Fuck, I don't have a condom with me," Max said.

"I have some in my bedroom."

"Bedroom it is. I'm not going to leave you here alone, you naughty girl."

Max helped me get up and placed his hands under my ass. I jumped on him. Max sauntered over to the kitchen door. I opened them and we went through the hallway into my bedroom. To my relief, Luna hadn't been waiting somewhere on the way.

I opened the door to the bedroom. Max walked in and turned left to lay me down on the bed. Then I hit something with my leg. It landed with a loud thud on the ground. I looked down. My handbag lay overturned on the floor. My porn folder was a foot or so away from the bag. "Larry the King of Porn Studios" was written on top of it in a big pink font.

I jumped off Max and crouched to collect the folder. Max caught my wrist and lifted my chin with his other hand.

"What is it?" He shook his head. "Please don't tell me you're going to work in porn."

"I… I'm not going to work there. I told them I wasn't interested."

"What the fuck is this?" Max said and pulled my naked photo from underneath the nightstand.

"Oh, shit."

Max stared at me with wide, frightened eyes. "What the fuck are you doing, Olivia?"

He brought the photo closer to his face. "It's not recent. What's that about?"

"Please sit down. I'll explain everything to you," I said.

He sat at the edge of the bed, still holding the picture in his hand. He shook his head. "Why did you hide it from me?"

"I didn't know they kept it. I was told it would be destroyed."

"When was this picture taken?"

"Over two years ago, before I started working as an escort. I was about to start working in porn when I spotted an opportunity to work as an escort."

"Why were you there today? Did you want to go back to your original plan?"

"I know, it was a mistake. I should have spoken with you before I went there. But at least I have the folder back."

"I don't know what to say, Olivia. Are you looking for trouble on purpose?"

"I need to make money. My mom is getting better, but I still want to help her move here. I need more money for that. But I realized today I couldn't do it at my expense. Not in porn."

"And at my expense, too. What if you started working there and someone sent the pictures or videos to me? Or worse, to your mom or your aunt? Would it be worth the money then?"

I hid my head in my hands and rubbed my temples. "I'm sorry, Max. It was reckless."

"No more hiding things from me, okay?"

"Okay. I'm sorry, Max. I just didn't want you to control my life, to tell me what job is good for me."

"I just want to know what's going on with you, to be a part of your life. That's the only way this partnership thing is going to work out, honey. And this thing with porn... I'm glad it turned out this way."

"I knew I made a mistake the moment I entered his office. I'm not going to see him ever again. Are you mad at me?"

He put a hand on my shoulder and massaged it. "It's okay, Olivia. Even when I have a really good reason to get angry at you, I can't. But I think that one of these pictures would help me forget about my anger."

"You're silly."

Max chuckled. "I don't need these. I'll take better ones with my own camera."

"Ooh, really?"

Max lifted my chin. "Write it down in your calendar, babe." He motioned with his head toward the folder on the floor. "I think you should get rid of this before Luna steals it from you."

"I know what to do with it."

I collected the folder and the pictures from the floor and grabbed Max's hand. "Come with me."

We went to the kitchen where I grabbed a box of matches. Then I guided Max to the living room and opened the patio door.

"Naked on your patio? You're getting adventurous, girl."

"It's dark. Nobody will see us. And I want to do this now."

I struck a match, grabbed the edge of the folder and set it on fire on the other edge. Max stood behind me and wrapped his hands around my waist. I looked at the burning folder like I was hypnotized. When the fire almost reached my hand, I tossed the folder away on the stones. The remaining part of the folder crumpled and blackened.

"So that's done," I said and turned around. I grabbed Max's hand. "Come on."

We went back inside and walked to the bedroom. I reached for my phone and loaded the contact list.

"Who are you calling?" Max asked.

"Nobody. Just getting rid of the old contacts." I brought the phone to Max's face and clicked delete on Victoria's name. Fiona's name went next. I also deleted the main number to the office. "Now everything is done."

"I'll help you get a regular job. We'll be all right," he said.

I sat at the edge of the bed. Max sat beside me and placed his warm hand on my naked thigh.

"I know. Time to grow up and start a normal career," I said.

"I can't even begin to tell you how happy I am to hear that."

"What about you, Max? I need to know about your plans."

"I'm not going to work as an escort anymore, if that's what you're asking. Striptease is not my kind of thing either. Let alone porn."

"I think you would do quite well in gay porn."

"Oh, do you?"

I laughed as Max laid me down on the bed and tickled me. His cock stiffened against my stomach and before I knew it, he sheathed his cock and slid inside me.

***

"So I was bored when you were away and checked some small hotels for sale in Mexico," Max said as we lay in the bed.

"Hotels for sale?"

"I remembered how you told me you'd like to run a small guest house. I turned my laptop on and checked some properties for fun. I think you'll really like some of them."

I loved how thoughtful Max had been. He seemed to remember every little detail I shared with him. "Send them over to me when you're back home. It's nice to visualize your dreams, right?"

"Let me grab my phone. I have them saved there. I can show you."

"There's a cable in my drawer. Upload them to my laptop."

"Okay."

I lay on the bed, enjoying the warmth of the bed and Max's scent in the air. I could get used to having this man by my side every single morning. But wasn't it too early to ask him about it? Max shook me out of my thoughts when he entered the bedroom with a phone in his hand. I glanced at his firm, naked body. Even though we had sex just a couple minutes ago, I was ready to go again. And probably again after that. And again.

I would bring his mouth to mine, let him slide his tongue over mine and suck my nipples.

"Which one?" Max asked.

I jerked and looked up. "Which what?"

"Which drawer, honey. I'm looking for the cable."

"The second one over there."

Max pulled out the cable and grabbed my laptop. He placed the computer on his legs and propped his back against the headrest. I joined him and leaned my head onto his shoulder.

"So here's the first one," he said. "Cozumel island. We were there for a couple hours."

"Yeah, I remember."

I loved the place. It looked like a tropical paradise, except for the huge cruises bringing hordes of tourists in like clockwork.

The photos featured a plot of land with palm trees and a beachfront two-story villa painted bright yellow. There were several hammocks tied to the trees, facing the turquoise Caribbean Sea. The interior was in a typical tropical design – a lot of wood, light brown and cream-colored furniture, and well-lit, spacious bedrooms.

It was a decent house, but definitely didn't match the mental picture of my perfect small guesthouse.

"It's okay," I said. "But nothing special."

"I get what you mean by that. I didn't find it perfect, either. And there's not really that much space for guests. Let me show you the next one."

The next pictures featured a small, two-bedroom house painted bright white. There were a couple smaller thatched roof cabanas on either side of the main house. There was a large swimming pool in the center of the area and a smaller swimming pool beside the main house.

The interior of the main house had a modern minimalistic design. I liked how spacious it was and how well the design worked with the blue sky outside and the emerald water in the distance.

"This one is a couple miles away from Puerto Morelos," Max said. "It was a small family resort. Not as close to the beach as the previous one, but still beachfront."

"It's really beautiful," I said. "Show me the pictures again."

"I knew you'd love it," he said and displayed the pictures again.

If only I had enough money, I would move there. Not alone, of course. I would take my mom, Luna and Max. Courtney and Tim could stay there on vacations.

"Are there more?" I asked.

"There's one more. I think I saw at least fifteen or so, but these three were the best ones."

"Show me. I doubt anything will be better than this one."

Max smiled. "We'll see." He opened the next set of pictures and I gasped.

"Oh, God. Did you take it straight from my head?"

"Maybe," he chuckled.

The last property consisted of a thatched roof, two-story house and several houses around it.

The main house had five bedrooms, two bathrooms and a huge kitchen – everything furnished with stylish, dated tropical furniture. I saw several things to fix, but I could see how beautiful it would look if renovated.

There were two living rooms, both of which opened to an enormous patio. A wooden pergola was partly shaded with large palm trees growing in the backyard. Under the pergola stood wicker lounge chairs and a handmade table that needed painting. A white-sand beach was just twenty or so yards away from the backyard.

A smaller one-story, two-bedroom house stood right beside the main building. It had the same interior design as the main building and its own small roofed patio.

Five smaller cabanas, all designed as luxuriously at the main house, were located fifty or so yards away. Each building faced the sea and had one bedroom, a small kitchen and sparkling white bathrooms.

"Where is it?"

"About thirty miles south of Tulum, the place with Mayan ruins."

"I remember."

"It's located near the Sian Ka'an biosphere reserve. There's a small town of Punta Allen about two miles south. It's off the beaten path."

"God, it's so beautiful. I wish I could live there. Is it for sale?"

"Yes, it is."

"Good. Call the owner and tell him to keep it for me. Maybe I'll buy it in twenty years."

"Maybe it will come true sooner thank you think."

"Yeah, if I inherit money from my long lost uncle in Nigeria. Hey, let me check my email. Maybe I got an email from his lawyer."

Max laughed. "You're funny." He leaned his face into mine and lightly kissed my lips. I parted them and brushed my tongue against his. Max brought me closer to his face and caressed my tongue with his.

"I love you, Max."

"I love you, too."

What a strange thing to come out of the mouth of an escort. No, I take it back. An ex-escort. This part of my life ended the moment I burned my old porn folder and did a sweep of my contact list.

As much as I wanted to avoid it, Max and Jamal were right. I needed to get a regular job and stop looking for an easy way out. I would start looking for it tomorrow.

Chapter 8

MAX

"Holy shit, this place is so beautiful, man," I said.

"I told you I had good contacts here," Jamal said.

It had been only a couple weeks since I had been to Mexico, but I already missed it. Each time I visited this place, whether I stayed in my usual hotel in Playa del Carmen or wandered down the coast, I felt as if I was back at home.

Olivia had made it obvious she also loved this part of this beautiful country. I was sure that if she saw what stood right in front of me, she would say it's beyond everything she had seen here so far.

Okay, I admit, it was a bit rundown and needed renovation, but I could already see its potential and how amazing it could look after repairs.

"Where's your guy?" I asked Jamal.

"He's coming. Should be here any minute. He told me to feel free to walk around the area."

"Then let's go." I felt like a kid in a candy store. I knew Olivia would be even more struck by how perfect this place was.

We walked around the main house and the smaller house that stood beside it. I looked through the windows inside both buildings. The furniture inside was the same as in the photos. So far, everything looked like it was presented in the online listing.

I sat down on a recliner on the patio that belonged to the smaller house. I decided it would be perfect for Olivia's mom. I had no doubt we could turn the place into a luxurious quiet retreat and support ourselves with it.

"Max," Jamal shouted. "Mauricio is here."

I resisted a chuckle when I saw Jamal's friend, the local real estate agent. I expected a man in his fifties dressed in a linen suit with a black leather suitcase in his hand. What I got instead was a man in his late thirties dressed in a white t-shirt, khaki shorts and flip-flops. He had shoulder-length dark hair and wore dark Aviators. His ride – a golf cart – was parked beside the main house.

"*Mucho gusto*," I said.

"Nice to meet you," he said with a strong Mexican accent. "Can I show you the house now?"

"Sure."

Two hours later, Jamal, Mauricio, his driver Esteban and I sat in lounge chairs on the main patio. Esteban was kind enough to drive to Punta Allen and grab us a couple cold bottles of beer while we inspected the property.

I knew I wouldn't find a better place than this one, and at such a great price at that. Mauricio was more than eager to negotiate with me, citing as the reason the long time he had been trying to sell the property. It was too far away from the main tourist places to draw the attention of real estate investors, and too expensive for local businessmen.

We went down to a price I could afford if I sold my house and Olivia sold hers. With my savings, we would still have enough money to renovate the property and live off that for at least a year. And if

Olivia's mom sold her house in Vermont, we would have much more time to properly market our little resort and get it off the ground. Jamal alone had enough contacts to bring the first clients.

"So, what do you think about it, Max? The price is good, the location is what you were looking for, and I'm the friendliest real estate agent in the country. What's there to think about? *Nada*."

I chuckled and patted Mauricio on the back. His relaxed attitude had always been one of the things I loved the most about this part of Mexico. Almost everyone who lived here had a positive outlook on life, so different from the permanent scowls on the faces of people I passed on the streets of Phoenix.

"Let me tie up a few things and I'll email you, okay?"

"That's fine, *amigo*. There's no rush. Let's enjoy the beer and the evening."

We checked out of the guest house in Punta Allen the next day. When we were on our way back to the Cancún airport, my phone rang. It was Olivia.

"Hey, honey. How's your trip?"

"Fine. I wish you were here with me. How are the interviews today?"

"Don't ask. I have one more in thirty minutes. I don't think I can stomach another hour sucking up to a fat guy in a suit."

I laughed. "You're a smart girl. No need to suck up. They would be stupid not to hire you."

"You're talking like I'm applying for a key position. It's just a boring sales rep job, Max."

"Shhh… You have to start with something, right?"

Olivia sighed. "It's just so difficult to switch."

"I know. But I'll be there for you. Trust me, it will be worth it."

Oh, if she only knew how much.

"Thanks, Max. Listen, I need to call a cab. It wouldn't do me good to be late."

"Sure. I'm standing in front of the airport. I gotta go, too."

"I love you, Max."

"Me too. See you in a couple hours, honey."

I hung up.

"Olivia?" Jamal asked.

"Yeah. Listen, Jamal, can you give me the number to your real estate agent in Phoenix? I want him to start looking for a buyer for my house."

"What about Olivia?"

"I want to have everything in place before I ask her. If the only missing piece is the sale of her house, she wouldn't have many arguments against doing it. You know how she can be sometimes."

"Yeah, unfortunately I do."

We laughed and walked into the airport.

OLIVIA

"We're willing to offer you a two-week trial period, Ms. Parker," Mr. Manhart said.

He was a man in his late fifties with all the worst perks of it – a gray receding hairline, a beer gut and probably clogged arteries, too.

He had a round-shaped face and sagging cheeks. I didn't find him particularly trustworthy for my first boss, but I didn't have much of a choice. The salary he offered me, especially with all the commissions I could generate, was much higher than I had expected. It was still nothing compared to what I made as an escort, but at least I wouldn't work for minimum wage.

"When do I start?"

"As soon as you're ready. Even tomorrow."

"Sounds good. I'm interested."

"Splendid. I'll send your documents over to the HR department. You'll work the first two weeks in our office and with our most experienced salesmen in the field."

And just like that, after sending seventy nine resumes and doing six interviews, I finally landed a job without 'getting naked' listed as one of the responsibilities. I guess I was one of the lucky ones, knowing how difficult it was to get a job.

I didn't have illusions – Mr. Manhart hired me for my tits, or at least that's how I felt after I caught him staring at them for the seventh time. But hey – a good appearance is an important perk during meetings with potential clients, right? My breasts could make him a lot of money.

I left the office building a couple minutes later and got into a cab. Thirty minutes later, I walked into my house. Luna greeted me at the doorstep and begged for food. I filled her empty bowl and went to the bedroom to get changed into more casual clothes. I realized my wardrobe had been full of sexy clothes, but virtually devoid of any professional ones – just a couple dresses and one pair of black trousers.

God, I hated this. Working as an escort wasn't one of the most reputable things to do, but at least I could dress in pretty clothes on a daily basis. Oh, and I could afford clothes whenever I wanted to improve my wardrobe. It had been two years since I last had to count money, and I didn't like it at all.

My phone rang.

"Hey, girl. Wanna hang out today? I have cool news to share," Courtney said.

"You're pregnant?"

She burst out laughing. "Not yet."

"Getting married?"

She chuckled. "Not yet. I'll tell you when I see you. Let's go to this new café."

"I'm spent, Courtney. Can we just stay at my place, have a coffee on the porch?"

"Okay. I'll be there in an hour."

"Works for me. See you."

I sat on my bed and sighed. Starting tomorrow, I wouldn't be able to meet with Courtney in the middle of the day. All kinds of social life would be off-limits until five PM, if not later. God, there were so many things about having a regular job that I hated.

Working as an escort had been almost like an addiction. When you get used to a high standard of living, it's hard to go back to living like a normal person. Hey, don't judge me. I had never been one of the rich pricks complaining about the softness of their towels. I just enjoyed my unconventional lifestyle, even if I had to hide what I did from almost everyone I loved.

Luna jumped on the bed and sat on my lap. I stroked the middle of her forehead and caressed her throat up to her chin. She craned her head in approval and purred for more. I laid back on the bed. Luna made herself comfortable on my stomach.

Two minutes later, I was deep asleep.

The loud ring of my phone woke me up an hour later. I jerked on the bed, tossing Luna off my stomach.

"Hello?" I said, half-conscious.

"Where are you? I'm at the doorstep."

"Oh, shit. I'm coming."

I rubbed the sleep from my eyes, pulled myself to my feet and plodded to the door. Courtney welcomed me with a wide smile on her face.

"You weren't kidding about the exhaustion," she said. "It's so unlike you to sleep in the middle of the day."

"Say hello to the new me, a sales rep for hygiene products."

"Congratulations." Courtney pulled me into her arms and rubbed my back. "This is good, isn't it?"

"I guess I should be happy."

"Hey, are we going to have coffee on your doorstep?"

"Oh, I'm sorry. Come on in."

I moved away from the door and let Courtney in. I sat in the kitchen chair and tried to wake up while she made coffee for both of us. Then we sat on the porch with cups of hot coffee cooling off at the small wooden table.

"So, what's the good news you wanted to share?" I asked.

"Tim and I are going to open a restaurant in three months."

I no longer needed coffee to wake up. I jumped from my chair and hugged Courtney.

"This is so fucking awesome," I said. "I'm so happy for you."

"Hey, it doesn't exist yet. You'll congratulate me when you order the first meal there."

I sat in the chair again and took a sip of coffee.

"What cuisine? What location? How large is it going to be?"

"We're pretty sure it's going to be a Thai restaurant. Tim has a friend who's a Thai chief looking for a new job. We can partner up with him."

"I'll be the first person to get some pad thai at your place. Don't even dare to open it before I sample your menu."

Courtney laughed. "You got it."

"What about... your job? What about Tim's?"

"That's why we're doing it. Tim spoke with Max a couple times. Max encouraged him to think long-term and reinvest his money in a proper business. It rubbed off on me, too."

I nodded. "Max the preacher. Are you going to miss your job?"

"Do you miss yours?"

"I'm probably stupid for saying this, but I do. I mean, I don't particularly miss the sucking cocks part, but I do miss the money and flexible work hours. I have to wake up at seven tomorrow to get ready for my new job."

"Oh, you poor thing. They hired you for a trial period, right?"

"Two weeks. Then they'll decide whether to keep me or let me go. I kind of hope they won't hire me."

"Then it's not the right job for you. You need to look for something that fits you. Something like the escort job, except for the cocks part."

"Easier said than done."

"Where would you like to work? I can ask around, see if someone can refer you."

"I always wanted to run a small hotel. I don't think you can help me with that, unless you have a million or two to share."

"Talk with Max. He's a smart guy."

"He knows it's my dream."

"Then sit down with him and think about how to achieve it. I have always dreamed about running my own restaurant. Now we found a way to do it. You'll figure it out, too."

Yeah, right. I learned a long time ago that life wasn't a fairy tale.

Chapter 9

OLIVIA

I stopped dead in my tracks. It couldn't be, but it was. Jack, the man who loved rough anal sex and unexpected facials stood by the desk, talking with a cute twenty-something blond secretary.

I hadn't thought about the consequences of my previous life while looking for a new job. Most of my clients were wealthy. Many of them were affluent because of a high-paid job in a corporation. I was bound to meet one of them sooner or later. The world was much smaller than I thought.

Jack was supposed to be the final pro sales rep I had to follow for a couple days to learn the trade. I was dressed in black trousers and a white dress shirt, an outfit that was far away from the sexy clothes I wore during my appointment with him. My hair was tied up in a professional bun. I almost couldn't recognize myself in the mirror. I hoped he wouldn't recognize me, either. After all, we only met for an hour a couple months ago.

I still wanted to hide in the bathroom and ask Mr. Manhart to assign me a different sales rep to follow. I was about to turn on my heels and disappear from Jack's view when he turned around and walked in my direction.

I watched his face and remembered his growls when he fucked me in the ass. He didn't seem to recognize me. He extended his hand and sent me a courteous smile. He had light stubble on his face and his brown hair was slightly shorter than I remembered. He also seemed to have gained a few pounds, bringing him closer to the "slightly overweight" territory.

"Hello, I'm Jack Garner. I presume you're Olivia Parker, my tagalong for the next three days?"

"I am. Nice to meet you, Jack."

A flash of recognition passed over his face. "Do we know each other?"

"I doubt it. Maybe we saw each other in the office a couple days ago?"

"No, I don't think so."

His phone buzzed. "Oh, I have a meeting in an hour. Come on, you're going to learn how to negotiate with a corporate client."

I followed him out of the building. I got into his gray Audi and turned my face away from him, pretending I was interested in watching the city.

He pulled onto the street and turned down the volume of the radio.

"Where did you work as a sales rep previously?"

"I have never worked as a sales rep."

"Any other sales experience? Retail?"

"No. It's my first job in sales."

"So, what's your job experience?"

His probing had been getting suspicious and reminded me more of an interrogation than a friendly small talk. I turned my head and looked at him. He shot me a brief glance.

"I worked in event planning."

A smirk appeared on his face. I didn't like it at all.

"Event planning, huh? I think I met you at one of the... events. In a hotel room a couple months ago."

I clutched the strap of my purse and counted to three. "It's possible. I had a couple events at various hotels. Maybe it was a conference for PHX Hygiene Cleaning Solutions."

"No, it wasn't. I remember it well, *Layla*."

He brushed his hand against my leg. I shifted on the seat, trying to make myself as small as possible and put more distance between us. Every inch counted.

"I don't know what you're talking about."

"Oh, you do. It was a shame I couldn't order you again."

"Mr. Garner, I think you're mistaken."

He pulled his car into a parking lot of a large office building. He turned the engine off, locked the door and turned his body toward me.

"Here's what I can offer you, Layla, Olivia, or however you want to be called. We're going to repeat what we did in the hotel. In return, I'm going to praise you in front of the boss."

"What if I don't want to do it?"

"Then I'll tell him you're a horrible employee and he would make a mistake hiring you. I'm his top performing sales rep. He listens to me."

"Why are you doing this?"

He ogled my body and pointed with his hairy hand at my tits. "That's why. I liked fucking you, Layla."

God, did I have 'escort' written on my forehead? Would I ever escape my previous life?

"I no longer work as an escort. Let me out."

"Why not consider it… a job responsibility? You can climb really high if I put in a good word for you."

"Let me out. I'm not interested."

"Think about it, Olivia. I'll make it possible for you to work for the company and get a quick promotion. Maybe you'll even be my personal assistant when I become the boss?"

I fumbled with the buttons on the door, but none worked to open it. "Let me out or I'll scream."

"I'm not a rapist, darling. I'm just giving you an option. If you're not interested, you might as well go home because Greg won't hire you."

"Unlock the door. I'm not interested."

He placed his hand on my thigh. "Honey, give it a thought. I'm sure you'll enjoy it." I slapped his hand and tossed it away. I punched him in the groin. He whimpered from pain as I reached for the button to unlock the door. The door clicked open. I left him writhing from pain in the driver's seat.

"Fuck you. I don't give a fuck about this job."

I took a cab home, tossed my purse in the corner and took off my professional clothes. They made me feel so queasy. I was done with the corporate life. Might as well try to fit a square peg in a round hole.

MAX

"We'll be in touch. I'll call you later this week with the answer," I said.

"Thank you. The buyer isn't in a huge rush, but I would appreciate your call as soon as possible."

"Of course. Have a good one, Howard."

133

"You too, Max."

I wanted to jump from joy and open a bottle of champagne. After less than two weeks of looking for a potential buyer I already had one, eager to close the transaction as soon as possible. All that was left to do was to talk with Olivia and unveil my surprise.

I called her cell. She picked up after the fourth ring.

"Hey, Max," she said in a tired, sad voice.

"What happened, honey?"

"Long story, but I lost my job."

"You have three days left of the trial period, right?"

"No more."

"What happened?"

"I don't want to talk about it over the phone."

"I wanted to come to your place, anyway. I can be there in thirty minutes."

"Fine."

Twenty five minutes later I parked in Olivia's driveway. I got out of the car and realized that unless I wanted to drive for almost two thousand and five hundred miles, I had to sell it. To hell with the Mercedes. I could ride a golf cart. I laughed to myself and knocked on the door.

"What's so funny? I saw you laughing on the way here," Olivia said. Sadness and irritation were written all over her face. I hoped it would turn into an expression of joy when I told her about my plan.

"I'll explain it later. Maybe you'll welcome me with a kiss or something, babe?"

She leaned in and kissed me. "I'm sorry. I had a bad day."

I walked into her house. We sat in the kitchen. The kettle was on. "Green tea as always," I said.

"I know."

"Tell me about your day," I said. "Tell me what happened with your new job." I wanted to know what I was dealing with before I delivered the good news.

"I was supposed to tag along one of the sales pros. He turned out to be one of my old clients."

I sighed. "That's bad."

"Not nearly as bad as what happened later. He told me that if we didn't repeat our appointment, he would make sure I wouldn't be hired."

"Fuck." I banged my fist on the table. "What is wrong with these people? I hope you kicked him in the balls."

"I punched him in the groin. Does it count?" Olivia said and poured the water into the mugs.

"I wish I was there with you. I would add my own compliments. What a fucking douchebag."

I would gladly beat the fucker, but he made it easier for me to share the news with Olivia. As Tim liked to say, 'there's always something good hidden in the bad.'

"I didn't like this job anyway. Don't be mad at me, but I'm glad I'm not going to work for them."

"Why would I be mad at you?"

"I can't be a corporate drone, Max. This life is not for me."

Olivia placed the mugs on the table and sat on the other side.

"Come here," I said and patted my knees. "I need to tell you something."

Olivia walked across the table and sat on my lap. "Please don't tell me it's something bad."

"Quite the contrary." I smiled. "Ready to hear it?"

She nodded. "Tell me."

"Do you remember that small hotel I showed you a couple weeks ago?"

"Which one? The one with a huge patio and a pergola?"

"Yes, this one."

"What about it?"

"Do you still want to own a hotel?"

Olivia raised her eyebrows and gazed at me with confusion. "What are you talking about, Max?"

"When I went two weeks ago to Mexico, I was there to inspect the property and speak with the agent selling it. I negotiated a really good price."

"I don't get it."

"I have a buyer for my house. I have some savings and I can sell my car. If you sell your house, we'll have more than enough to buy this place and renovate it."

"Oh my God, Max. Please don't tell me it's a joke."

"It's not a joke. I need to make two phone calls and it's going to be our new reality."

"No way." Olivia stared at me with huge eyes. She was so adorable I wanted to carry her to the bedroom and rip off her clothes. "Are you serious?"

"I took care of everything in the past few weeks. All I need is your 'yes.' I know it's a big move, but w—"

"Yes. Yes. Yes. God, Max, there's nothing more in the world I want than to start over somewhere else and pursue my dream."

"The smaller house beside the main house would be perfect for your mom. We can help her sell her house in Vermont and she could move in there with us."

A tear trickled down Olivia's cheek. "I love you so much, Max."

Epilogue

TWO YEARS LATER

OLIVIA

"I will never get enough of fucking you in the shower," Max said as he dried his body with a towel. God, I craved him even more with each day. The Mexican sun had worked miracles on his already tanned and muscular body, making it even more defined and delicious.

"You're lucky Mom's playing with Daniel."

"Oh, the joys of parenthood."

I slapped him on the arm and laughed. He pulled me in and gave me a long, passionate kiss.

"If she wasn't, I'd get Tim or Courtney to do it," he said. "Vacation isn't only about drinking margaritas and enjoying the sun. They should share some of the responsibilities."

"Oh, give them a break, honey. They've been working hard with the launch of their second restaurant."

I heard Daniel's voice coming from the patio. "You better get dressed. Our break is over," Max said.

"Honeymooners from Vancouver will be here soon, too." I said.

"And I have a massage in fifteen minutes."

I chuckled. "Tim and Courtney it is, after all."

I pulled on my shorts, put on my bra and kissed Max. We left the bathroom. Mom carried Daniel in her arms. Over a year and a half later, I still couldn't believe how strong and healthy she had become after the surgery. Gone was the frail woman, and in her place was a vibrant, always smiling person who managed our cleaning team. Even carrying our twenty pound son wasn't a problem for her.

"Who's standing there, baby boy?" Mom said. "It's your mommy and daddy."

"Hi, Daniel," I said and took Daniel in my arms.

"Mommy," he said.

Max stroked Daniel's head. "Daddy," Daniel said.

"Daddy needs to go to work, son," Max said.

My husband leaned in to kiss me. Mom watched us with a wide smile on her face. At moments like this, I felt as if I had been living in a fairy tale. And to think that none of this would happen if Lex hadn't come up with her crazy idea.

"I better split, honey. Need to get ready for the massage," Max said.

"Don't flirt with her," I said.

"Oh, as if there were any woman who's even half as perfect as you are."

Max left our house through the patio and stroked Luna, who lay on her back on a recliner in the sun. The doorbell rang. I glanced at the clock and realized it was past three. Our new guests were on time.

"Mom, could you carry him to Tim and Courtney? You should take a break. I need to take care of the guests."

"I can take care of him. Let them rest."

I glared at her. "You should rest. Daughter's orders."

"Okay, okay." She smiled and took Daniel from my arms.

I walked to the door and opened it. A beautiful couple in their late twenties stood at the doorstep with huge smiles on their faces. They looked around our property with awe. I didn't think it would ever get old to see the faces of our new guests enchanted by our little luxurious retreat.

"Welcome to Casa Olivia. Let me take you to your cabana."

Subscribe to C. L. Porter's Mailing List

Sign up for my newsletter at http://eepurl.com/_VtsL to receive exclusive updates about incoming titles and to be the first to get your hands on the new releases (including free advance reader copies for readers willing to write a review).

Books by C. L. Porter

Addicted to Lawyers Trilogy

My name is Julia, and I was addicted to sex with lawyers. In their offices. During our appointments.

The story you're about to read will give you a glimpse into my weird addiction from the day it began up to the day it ended. If you have ever wondered how it feels to flirt with random strangers and make them squirm just minutes later, I will satisfy your curiosity.

At Your Service

I'm Olivia. I'm twenty-five, and I've been working as an expensive call girl under the pseudonym Layla for two years. The job involves a lot of hard work (pun intended), but the money is worth it. And then one day I receive a text from my boss that throws my life upside down…

I'm Max. I'm twenty-five, and I've been working as a male escort for older women for three years. My clients know me as Ethan. Recently I've been having problems getting it up during my appointments (shhh, don't tell anyone). When I break one of my most important rules to return a favor, my life gets even more difficult...

Copyright 2015 by C. L. Porter.

Reproduction in whole or part of this publication without express written consent is strictly prohibited.

This is a work of fiction. Names, characters, places and incidents either are the product of the author's imagination or are used fictitiously, and any resemblance to actual persons, living or dead, business establishments, events or locales is entirely coincidental.

***

Please consider leaving a review or spreading the word to support the author.

Made in the USA
Columbia, SC
25 June 2021